Mr. Aartemann's

CRAYON

Alan Daugherty

Mr. Aartemann's
CRAYON

TATE PUBLISHING & *Enterprises*

TATE PUBLISHING
& Enterprises

Tate Publishing is committed to excellence in the publishing industry. Our staff of highly trained professionals, including editors, graphic designers, and marketing personnel, work together to produce the very finest books available. The company reflects the philosophy established by the founders, based on Psalms 68:11,

"THE LORD GAVE THE WORD AND GREAT WAS THE COMPANY OF THOSE WHO PUBLISHED IT."

If you would like further information, please contact us:

1.888.361.9473 | www.tatepublishing.com

TATE PUBLISHING & *Enterprises*, LLC | 127 E. Trade Center Terrace

Mustang, Oklahoma 73064 USA

Cover design by Elizabeth Mason
Cover photo by Alan Daugherty with digital enhancement by Deric Daugherty
Interior design by Janae J. Glass
Illustration by Alan Daugherty

Published in the United States of America
ISBN: 978-1-5988685-2-4

07.02.06

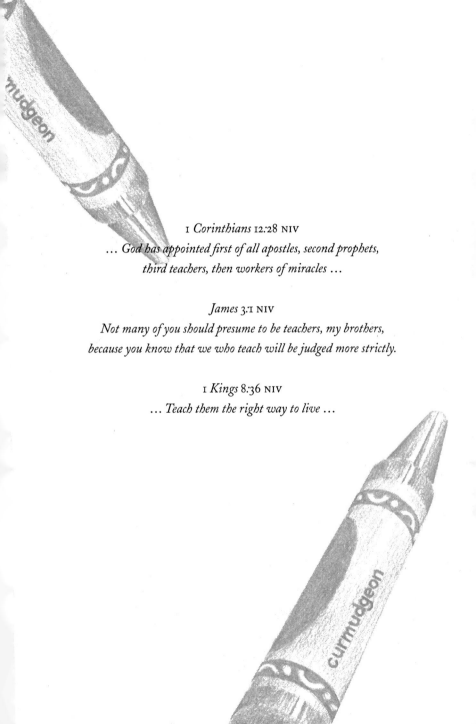

1 Corinthians 12:28 NIV
… *God has appointed first of all apostles, second prophets,
third teachers, then workers of miracles …*

James 3:1 NIV
*Not many of you should presume to be teachers, my brothers,
because you know that we who teach will be judged more strictly.*

1 Kings 8:36 NIV
… *Teach them the right way to live …*

Dedication

Mr. Aartemann's Crayon is prayerfully and lovingly dedicated to my champion of faith, encouragement, confidence, and love—my wife, my life—Gwen.

Additionally, I dedicate this book to my prayer support that comes from my Sunday school class at Hope Church, whose prayers I truly believe are the reason for every breath I am able to breathe.

Disclaimer

Not only have all the names been changed to protect the innocent but it can be questioned if any of the characters really exist. The author receives senior discounts without asking and is quite forgetful but never lets that interfere with what he passes on as reality. If you recognize any character or event or location in this story you may assume it is a nightmare and not the same as the actual event, person, or otherwise that you are familiar with. If something seems so ridiculous and preposterous that it is quite unbelievable then that may or may not have some slight correlation to the author's lifestyle. If you recognize a character as being something like yourself anyplace in this book, please write the author that we may pray for each other. If you discover delight or ministry in these pages it was flagrantly intentional.

Contents

Character List

Mr. Aartemann	art instructor
Mrs. Ruth	a kindergarten teacher
Abby Beatrice Sledford "Abs"	school counselor
Edward (not his real name)	a kindergarten leader
Ms. Mopp	a substitute custodian
Yancy Cain	fifth grade student
Gail Aartemann	Aartemann's wife
Mrs. Francis Peiper	kindergarten teacher
Janet Neuenschwander	fifth grade teacher
Dorothy Best	first grade teacher
Paul Williams	Abs boy friend
Miss Cable	school librarian
Principal Gene	principal of the elementary
June Long	third grade teacher
Cindy	a teacher
Jill Schwartenbarger	school office secretary
James	Aartemann's fictitious name of the former secretary

Introduction

I grew up in a family that had a meager lifestyle and income. Enough was provided that I never considered the fact that we might be classified poor by some standards. I was born a Hoosier and lived several years on the family farm. Few people my age experienced growing up without indoor plumbing, that modern feature achieved finally in the twelfth year of my life. At that time we moved next door to my only living grandparent.

I grew up expecting to work and provide for some of my own wants. Lawn mowing and farm labor during school years provided desired spending money. At one time my brother and I (two in a family of six siblings) cut grass on literally half the lots in the small town where we lived. This included the church lot where we attended. Employment allowed me to buy my first car, a ten-year-old Olds, and my way through college. Our family church was next door to our house so as a youth; only severe illness was an excuse for not attending any and every meeting at the church. The Lord being our provider and strength was ingrained very early in life. That came to be tested in adult years.

Grief from death, fear from illnesses, and an automobile accident with painful recovery forced continuing looks inward upon the faith that was built upon the foundation of Godly and praying parents. In desperation to hang on to a lifelong belief in the goodness of God, the writing process was reluctantly rekindled. It began when life seemed to be summed up simply by the one word—void. The fire inside never died completely but the uncontrollable path that my life was on seemed far distant from what I believed the God of my Christian faith would have for me. Joy had passed. Life was so devastated that even continuing to ask why became useless thought and prayer.

A childhood Christian foundation kept me seeking His face. Others prayed and encouraged the search. I read. I meditated. I worshiped at church and privately at home. I listened to Christian music as loud as the player could produce it. I prayed, sometimes hours at a time. I cried, sometimes hours at a time. I even finally began to write. One friend suggested putting down just a word or an incomplete sentence indicating any positive that happened in a day. I tried, but some days were blank. Eventually the hopelessness lessened. Finally, to my utter surprise, I startled myself with a laugh. The healing began and the writing continued—it was therapy. Writing became another form of worship. Christ's joy returned a bit at a time until I found laughter again within my life. It materialized in journal entries. The words were meant for my own needs. God was in the process. Blessed thoughts came as bursts of inspiration during writing hours.

Ultimately, a whole new avenue of writing began merely for the enjoyment of writing. Every now and then a portion was shared with family, colleagues, friends, or just my wife. Other segments were still kept private, like a confidence between best friends. The Lord opened up new avenues of life I never dreamed possible. Joy I felt at one point I would never achieve again, infiltrated me.

God alone knew the path I was to walk, the hardships I had and would face, but He also knew the strength He would supply to persist.

More than one doctor tagged me a "survivor" and one even used the word "miracle." I had a new life and it was filled with joy and laughter. Prayer had worked its miracle. I had changed, even seeming abnormal to some old friends. New and different paths were opened to me once I began riding in the backseat and allowing Jesus to guide my steering wheel. That was not an easy step since I had years of experience teaching driver training classes in addition to art education. Holding fast to the Lord's prompts was often complicated when, on occasion, family, friends, and colleagues questioned my new priorities and lifestyle changes.

The writing took a new road again, and pieces began aligning. Mr. Aartemann came into being as a fictional art teacher trying with all his earthly might to lead a life accountable to the Lord. He was a sinner when his fictional character was birthed.

Even today Aartemann is a sinner, but a repentant one, saved by Calvary and forgiven for his shortcomings. He lives a life that one moment has him spilling his coffee over the humorous words or actions of his classroom, and the next instant finds him in prayer or tears from the suffering of a student over matters that a child should not have to face. Mr. Aartemann somehow feels the same muscle pains that I, as his author, feel. He apes both my desires to minister to students in need and celebrate with them in their successes. He suffers from the retirement decision process just as his father did and just as this author's father did, and just as I do. He seeks the Lord's face and wisdom—as I do.

Mr. Aartemann's broken crayon is placed at rest and he prays at his desk.

"Lord, I wish to serve You doing the tasks that You desire under the power that You supply. Lord, if I can be of the most service to Your plan, if I can continue being a minister to the minds of children, if I can be an inspiration or demonstrate some moments of walking through life with You as core, center, and guide—then I will work on. I will remain in the classroom, survive the pains, attend the meetings, and try to be lead by You. But also Lord, give me a sign; if You would rather that I moved on in my life, and that a younger, healthier, more energetic art teacher should take my place. My will is to follow Your plan. Show me the way. Teach me Your will. *Give me a sign!* Lord, please give me a sign. Amen."

God Winds

It seems like such a time waster to read through a class list at the beginning of every class. But it is so necessary. It is his way in the first days of school with students. Two teacher days and a few student days proceeded today. They should have been labeled administrator days since meetings orchestrated by non-teachers took up most of the time that originally was to be for preparation and classroom set up. Teachers want to get ready on the teacher days. Some administrators assume every teacher had all summer to do that. Few consider that the contract doesn't allow for any paid summer preparation days. Most teachers donate several days, and the public thinks they get paid. Computer problems abound as well as abundant changes in class roster. That class list information takes a while in production.

The class lists, once finally secured, are not always updated to the intended accuracy needed to create seating charts used in an art classroom. Some students use abbreviated forms of their first name. These are never acknowledged on a computer entry in the school system. Others, like Danny, grow up to a Dan or Daniel over the summer. Others still have used their middle name so long that they do not even respond to the official given name. But "official" is the name on the list. Then there is the pronunciation challenge for Mr. Aartemann. He is a teacher servicing several hundred art students. So he faces the students on this first class meeting after receiving the list, nearly two weeks late—a record of sorts. The list is read prior to the seating chart creation. That seating chart will be Aartemann's job for next week.

He suggests a change from his traditional seating chart process. It's today's second group, a third grade class. Normally he has simply used some form of alphabetical grouping. It's not very creative for someone paid to teach creativity. Alphabetical plans allow shifting blame for students being assigned a seat beside someone not their best friend. Heaven forbid sitting beside the opposite sex. When that happens alphabetically it must be attributed to their parents for giving them their last name.

Their only alternate solution is to go to court and have their name changed. They could get adopted! Or get married. All are less than favorable options to elementary students. But, when they are verbally given the options it usually produces a laugh, a quiet eye roll, or a stare of dumbfoundedness. Student age is the primary factor in determining whether the joke gets a laugh. Today the joke seems to have aged quicker and in years beyond Aartemann's age. The discomfort of sitting beside the opposite sex also diminishes beyond the elementary ages quite rapidly. Teacher strategy reverses at those higher-grade levels.

Mr. Aartemann suggests to the class the placing of each student's name on a tiny slip of paper and dropping them in front of the large four bladed Patton Electric floor fan. Seats could then be assigned by where the slips floated to the tables. It was just a spur of the moment joke referring to the noisy fan operating necessarily. This school building was constructed in the twenties or thirties of the last century. It has no air conditioning luxury like the newer educational facilities. The worn brick building holds more heat on the first days of school than when the questionable boilers are attempting to create winter heating.

"Instead of blaming your parents' last name for your assigned seat you will have to blame God for where your name slip floated and dropped," he informs the students of the class.

Can I say God is Aartemann's knee jerk silent self interrogation. Or did he speak aloud? He really does not know. That's an Aartemann quirk.

"God doesn't make the wind, the air does," a student suddenly expresses over the murmuring of all those trying to guess if the art teacher is serious.

It is dangerous to make any statement in jest to elementary students of any age. They are so innocent and trusting. More than likely they will believe what is stated in its entirety regardless of how preposterous it may truly be.

Unfortunately, public school laws do not allow Aartemann to respond to the student's remark like he would prefer. The reality comment about God not making the winds is directed to the fact that the bulk of the wind going through the art room is not from the almost unnoticeable wisps through the window. The winds are generated by metal and a motor. Electric wind!

Since it is rather obvious the student is referring to natural wind, he wants in the worst way to be able to depart from the art lesson and discuss the relationship of God in nature. God is in air that is at rest. Aartemann wants to express his belief in God as the creator of all, including the wind.

Aartemann's faith wants to share from the first Genesis chapter: "So God made the expanse from the water above it. And it was so. God called the expanse 'sky.'"

What a lead-in that could be for continuing into the role of wind upon the history related in the Bible. Ultimately the Biblical wind was from the presence of the Holy Spirit given to those who accept the sacrifice of Jesus Christ, His death upon Calvary for every sin, and His victory over death—also a gift promised to all believers.

There was a time when teaching that tangent from a classroom student's comment would have been acceptable in the United States. Perhaps one day it will be again. Earlier this morning the school joined together in the nation's pledge. At one time that was also outlawed in certain places, even in schools.

The art teacher thought to himself, *I will continue to obey the law. I'll share my Lord by example. I'll pray that students come to understand the awesome power of wind—the wind of God. I can pray. I have that right. I will, before school, each day. I will pray for the Holy Spirit's wind to guide my seating assignment selections to what will best help each student. And I will pray that the Holy Spirit's wind will pass over each soul. I can silently do that! Ah, the wind of the Holy Spirit … it's electrical!*

The list is read, names corrected when needed, additions penciled in, and even two struck off. One deletion is due to a no-show student after nearly two weeks. The other, sadly, is due to a young girl being sent to live with her other parent for a spell. Now she lives in another state, a transfer of human goods that took place more than once with this child in the preceding school year. Aartemann places the list on his desk awaiting seating chart decisions. He chooses a couple of eager students to hand out the art projects already started from the class meeting of last week.

"Can you read names?" he asks a boy waving his hand so vigorously that he is in danger of lift off.

With the nod of his head, Aartemann first presents and then suddenly pulls the half stack of drawings from the young outstretched hand.

"Do you know everyone?" Aartemann questions further.

Getting another nod the papers are offered again. Again they are snatched back at the last minute before the youth can grasp a hold.

"Are your hands clean?"

Followed is another nod, another offer of the group of projects, and again the sudden withdrawing.

"Are you Republican?" is the next teacher query.

This causes a change from the smile of the lad to a pensive, pondering stare. A couple of chuckles erupt across the room from a pair that seems to know the meaning of the word Republican. Aartemann again, within his mind, wonders if he has stepped past a sacred don't-go-there school line. He hands the boy the stack with no further comment. Now he has to shake the stack in a gesture that indicates to the boy that finally he really gets to take them for distribution to the class. Aartemann turns to another blond headed overweight boy in the next chair at the same work table. He offers the other half of projects to him but pulls back his hand again at the last moment.

"Can you read, too?" he asks.

The blond nods.

"Can you read names?"

The toe-headed lad nods immediately.

"Do you know everyone?" Aartemann asks while all the time the boy with the quarter inch blond butch cut nods away continuously.

"Are your hands clean?" the teacher asks, watching the unstoppable nodding that the student is sure is a good idea until all the questions are completed.

"Are you a Republican? Is the ocean wet? Does the flag have stars? Did you bring me a Snicker's candy bar? Are your shoes tied?"

The boy looks at the Velcro straps on his shoes while still nodding affirmatively all the while. Aartemann releases his grip on the projects and the smiling lad stands. He heads toward the seat of the student whose project is on the top of the stack.

Aartemann goes to his desk just a couple of steps away and pointing to the blond boy doing the passing of the projects, states, "When you're done put the Snicker's bar on my desk please."

The class laughs at the trick. The lad grins in a way that looks like "Oops!" He peers down in a bit of embarrassment, and sees again his Velcro shoes. He is caught twice in one nod.

Aartemann works at his desk on the computer while the class goes about their own creative work. The students assume he is deciding upon their assigned seat. At the end of class Aartemann offers to the blond boy a chance to keep the Snicker's bar if he will pick up all of the projects in the room. The student grins and jumps at the chance to be the helper once again. The relief on his face demonstrates that he may have really thought he'd have to come up with a candy bar for Mr. Aartemann. Neither of the two will now know if the teacher would have actually accepted it if the child ever brought a Snicker's to school.

Aartemann types away on the computer. He is actually composing a letter to the administration, school board, superintendent, principal, and whoever else needs a copy when he is done. He is at an age and a time in his life when he is considering an end to his art teaching career. Is it time for a change? Is he ready for retirement? Has he stayed too long? Last year had felt like it at the end of the year. This year started out with as much stress and confusion as the ending of that now past year. Can he go on? Should he make this the last? It is time for a decision because knowing every day, every month, every grading period that it would be the last time—well, it will all be easier to finish the next eight months. The short-timer's count down could begin. Loops could be cut off a paper chain, just like counting down to Christmas vacation.

He ponders the words in the letter. Should he give a reason for leaving? He will be retiring earlier than a typical retirement age? Should he thank them? Who should he thank? What should he say first? He'd been working on the single computer page during the last half of the just released class. So far all he has is a heading, a blank space left for a date, and the words "Dear Sirs." Is "sirs" politically correct for a school board that has a couple of ladies sitting? Is the word "dear" too familiar, too unprofessional, sissy, or (good heavens) is it spelled right?

"Is it deer or dear?" he asks himself, so suddenly confused that simple words are questioned. Neither spelling looks correct to him. His query is audible.

Oh dear, deer, dere! he mentally utters just as he is saved by the sound of tiny feet and muttering voices of tiny children, and a not so tiny "sh-sh-sh" coming from a kindergarten teacher. She leads a straggling mass of wee bodies toward another class of art. Aartemann jumps to his feet glad to be free from his letter task. His hand salutes the incoming talkative tykes looking for someplace to sit. He gives a thumbs up to the first child taking a seat. The classroom teacher drifts away, the students roam about selecting a chair for another seventy-seven seconds until all are seated, and finally Mr. Aartemann states in his best booming art teacher voice.

"Welcome!"

Simultaneously with the welcome word the lights go black as a lightning bolt cracks outside. A softer rumble follows it like timpani behind symbols.

"Well, that takes care of the letter," Aartemann says aloud with no understanding from the young students.

Child eyes are now wide toward the ceiling and for some toward the windows. Aarteman hears the computer restarting as the lights flicker back on.

"We're having a hurricane!" speaks up a semi-frightened girl, wide-eyed at the rain on the windows. She wears a pretty yellow dress trimmed with some lace on the short sleeves and hems. A matching ribbon is in her springy curls. Her look is more like Shirley Temple heading to the Easter parade except for the bright pink rubber rain boots she still has on her feet. They are likely the only foot wear she has with her for the day.

Aartemann goes to her aid. He stoops beside her chair, and reassures her.

"No, no, no. It's just a rain storm. We don't have hurricanes here. We're lucky, aren't we? No, it's no hurricane, just some rain for the grass and the corn. Do you like corn on the cob? I do! I like it with lots of butter and salt and pepper. Do you like butter? Do you like pepper?"

With the food questioning the fear leaves the little girl's eyes. A smile comes over her face and he stands again to address the class.

"Girlz-z don like papper," Curly Temple, or whatever her name is, corrects him.

"Oh, you're absolutely right. Sorry!" Aartemann answers. She giggles. Her missing two teeth visually relate to her speech. One gap is causal.

The fear is real. Florida has just had a hurricane the day before and the news is constant on TV. Most students watch TV a lot and are thus informed on tragic current events of the world. Unfortunately, news reports are often misunderstood when youth get no adult assistance at home in understanding the entire video horror broadcast as breaking news. So the fear is real.

"I'm going to give you a seat just for your own today. Can you remember it till next week?"

Many nods wisp the air all around the classroom. Aartemann moves quickly into the normal routine to keep the minds off hurricanes.

"I'll point to a chair with this computer duster and if it is your name you may stand up and walk to the chair and sit down on the lap of the person sitting there now."

Students giggle a bit.

"No, no, no that will never work. Let's try this procedure. I'll point to a chair, you walk to the chair, and the person there already will then stand up till they hear their name. Now listen carefully. Listen pleas-s-s-se! Everyone be very quiet so you can hear the names. We'll start right here ..." he said, pointing to a chair. "Travis Keidler."

There is no movement.

"Travis Keidler?"

"I didn't sit there," responds a taller than average round—faced boy wearing a t-shirt a size or two large, likely a hand-me-down.

"I know. You see, I'm assigning seats today. This is your assigned seat starting today."

Then Aartemann realizes quickly that kinders will likely not understand the meaning of assigning seats.

"Travis, please sit here for me. This is the special seat I picked for just you. I'd like you to sit close to my desk in case I need some help."

That seems to do the trick as the lad gets up and moves to the empty chair.

"Very good! Thank you. Now in this chair ... Samuel Keller."

A boy across the room gets up slowly while staring first at the floor, and then begins moving as he rubs his eyes with a fist.

"I—I don't wan' ta sit there," he sniffles out softly. "I was sitting over here. I don't wan' ta sit there (sniff)."

"Oh my, you're not in trouble. I'm just giving everyone a special seat so I can take attendance from the seating chart, not punishment. You're going to sit in alphabetical order."

Suddenly he realizes the boy may not understand the words attendance, punishment, alphabetical order or seating chart. He rubs the boy's shoulder as he sits down in the new location. Aartemann's voice nearly breaks as he sees the child put his face in his arms and cry. Mr. Aartemann has a grandson that started kindergarten in another state just last week. He wonders if he cried in his art class. Feeling badly he is forced by time to continue on with the seat assignment task leaving the boy to overcome on his own.

By the time seating is assigned through all the six tables, four children to a work table in alphabetical order, Samuel has his head up and eyes again dry. Aartemann points to the space between Samuel and Travis and asks them, "Can I sit between you, right there, if I want to work on art like you do? Can I sit at your table?"

"We'll scoot over and you can sit in the middle," Samuel smiles as he responds to the teacher and demonstrates moving his chair.

His fine set of teeth all show through the huge grin.

The art teacher then looks up at the ceiling. His hand scratches his head. Looking puzzled he thumps his forehead. He informs the students eager to draw that he has forgotten what the project is for the day. He strolls searching the room informing the class he is looking for his thinking cap.

"I'm old, and old people forget, and I have a hat to help me remember … I forget where I put the hat."

Just then he stumbles over a big cardboard box. It is lifted up. A finger points to large red marker letters on the side. The students read in unison.

"H—a—t—s."

"Hats!" a bright kinder shouts from the green table after the spelling ends.

"Maybe my thinking cap, my thinking hat, is in here."

He pulls out a totally flat straw hat. The students laugh as he tries to put on the smashed hat unsuccessfully.

"Say some magic words for me," Aartemann encourages.

The students comply with all sorts of possibilities. He pops open the folded hat, and slams it in one continuous motion onto his head. It is a large straw cowboy hat that has a sagging brim covering both ears. Students all over the room offer suggestions as to the type of hat it is. Aartemann pretends he cannot hear.

"What?"

With that question the students' volume increases twofold.

"What?" Aartemann repeats the question.

Now the students are shouting.

"What?"

As the students try to be heard he lifts one flap and jumps vertically. He shakes his head. He sticks a finger in his ear and wags away the supposed ringing. With a finger to his lips during a "Sh—h," he immediately quiets the class.

"This isn't a thinking cap but it reminds me about active listening. You're doing a great job of active listening. That means you are quiet, not playing or touching anything on the table, looking at me and listening with your eyes and ears. That is important to learn. Every day you will have to do that to find out what we're going to make. Active listening, and you are doing it just right."

The next hat he pulls from the box is red plastic.

"That's a fireman's hat," is the unison response from nearly every student.

"Right! It's not a thinking cap at all. But it reminds me of something else. Firemen help us to be safe. We need to be safe in the art room. That means we don't throw anything—not pencils, crayons, not scissors, not even a cotton ball. Even a cotton ball can hurt if you get hit in the eye. We don't run in the art room, running is for the gym during P. E. class. We don't stand on the chairs, we don't walk on the walls, and we don't hang from the light fixtures," Aartemann rattles off fast as he ends up paused and pointing to the lights overhead.

The room breaks into a roar of kinder laughter. Many try to explain to the art teacher that they can't reach the lights at all. Most continue to giggle.

He puts away the red plastic fireman's cap and puts on a tall striped stovepipe hat.

"Cat in the Hat," the students shout.

"*No!*" Aartemann answers as he turns the hat inside out and states, "There's no cat in this hat."

"Cat in the Hat!" Samuel shouts jumping up and down beside his new seat.

The no-more-tears Samuel obviously, like the others, is referring to the book of that title.

"Cat in *the* Hat!" the students repeat, with Aartemann only shaking his head discarding the striped hat.

He shows a look of confusion.

"This isn't a thinking cap," he explains.

The obvious wrong hat is a golden glittered top hat often used by chorus line dancers. He grabs his umbrella, staged handily nearby for the occasion, and does a few bad dance steps first to the right and then back.

"It's a dancing hat," he says. "And I'm a terrible dancer."

While the students are still laughing at the silly dance, he removes the gold glittering hat. At the same time he takes great care to keep the hidden duplicate but sparkling silver hat on his head. The two hats stack together perfectly for the trick. He turns to face the class. Frantic elementary students are already shouting and pointing and laughing about the hat still on his head.

"It's still there. You still have a hat on your head," they shout.

Shaking his head again, he holds up the gold top hat causing them to point and more loudly try to assure the teacher that a hat remains. He dramatically looks wide—eyed and upward with his eyes going crossed. They point. He reaches over his head but missing the hat, feels nothing. They all shout that it is lower. Finally his hands touch the silver hat on top his head and he jumps off his feet in mock surprise. They laugh harder. He slowly takes hold of the brim of the silver hat and then suddenly lifts it off and looks up cross-eyed again.

"Is there another one?" he asks over the jovial noise.

"No," is the answer, twenty-four times, once by every student.

He has another silly hat to make them laugh. For this hat's lesson he then reminds them it is not nice to laugh at a person that is not trying to be funny. It's not nice to laugh and make fun of their art work. It's ugly to say nasty things and call names and do put downs. When people do and say ugly things then they usually do ugly art. When students say and do nice things for each other then they always do nice art. And a lesson will be remembered from the silly hat that has flowers and pigtails formed of pantyhose. That is also not a thinking cap.

This teacher/performer is at his peak. He thrives on the laughter and it encourages his teaching of his classroom procedures that serve as guides for the rest of the children's lives. At least that is Aartemann's prayer. He knows he can't make them all professional artists but he can help guide them to productive and pleasant adulthood. The art teacher prays for that ability, that power.

A nice dress hat is found in the box.

"This is my super best hat," he states. "I wear this when I want to look my super best, like going to church, or to someplace important like that. It reminds me! I ask you to do your super best in art class. Is anyone going to come to the art room to make the ugliest picture that you can? Of course not! Just work hard. Just do the best that you can do. You will have a lot of fun and do a lot of work. You will make many very nice things. Don't say 'I can't do that.' Instead say 'I've never done that before but I'm going to do my super best.' Okay? Super best! This isn't a thinking cap but I'm glad it reminds us all to do our super best in school, even in art class."

He picks up a wig out of the box and the students cackle hysterically. Then he actually puts it on his head and the laughter volume echoes off the high ceiling. He shushes the class quickly with a finger to the lips. That gesture is followed by a hand "L" sign representing active listening. He drops the wig into the box. Next quickly out is pulled a shower cap. As quick as Billy the Kid's draw it covers his hair. The laughter noise immediately blasts off. Again with the hand signal, the laughter ends as fast as it started.

With only two minutes to go in the class time, Mr. Aartemann apologizes for talking the whole time during art. He promises if the kindergarten kids can remember where their seat is next week he will not talk the whole time and they will make a picture. They promise. Upon lining up at the door and their teacher's return each tries to tell her about art class. A pair of dozen simultaneously explain how Mr. Aartemann couldn't find his thinking cap. Kinders tell their teacher that the art man talked the whole time. They are laughing; talking, giggling, smiling, reminding each other what had happened and leaving empty handed after a class of art but do not care. They leave the room having spent an entire period learning the procedures of the art room. Future life will be a bit sweeter for it.

The last student out of the room is Samuel and he turns at the door just before exiting and gives the thumbs up sign to Mr. Aartemann. He returns it with a smile as big as Samuel's. Again Aartemann prays his grandson will not have to cry in art class. Finally he remembers the unsaved letter lost to cyberspace due to the power outage.

"Later, much later," he speaks loudly to none around to hear.

Mr. Aartemann exits the school with Mrs. Ruth, the kindergarten teacher, at the end of the day. She's young. If he had a daughter she'd be that age. She is tall and slender, with a look about her. Every one of her students must wish she was their mother. She has only one child at home, but a room full at school. She's what every kindergartner should have for a teacher. He hopes his grandson has a Mrs. Ruth.

"I was outside your art room door in the hall about the last five minutes of my kids' art class. I was early to pick them up and just waited. I love to hear my kids laugh."

His truck door slams and he begins talking aloud once again to none but himself, "This morning I was ready to stop. Now I don't know. Is it time to stop teaching? Am I still needed? Is it time to move on in life? Later, much later! I better not get in a hurry. Think it through Aartemann, think it through. No haste. Think!"

The religious radio station comes on when the truck starts up with the turn of the key in his hand.

"Ah, week two is done. I should make a paper chain to count down to Christmas."

There is no one to agree or disagree.

One Square at a Time

He meets her at the walk leading from the faculty/staff parking area. It provides a dry cement path. The grass area is faster—as the bird's fly. The direct grass route is usable in dry conditions but not this day. The previous day's rainfall and the overnight addition to already soaked ground left the abundant bare areas looking like brown throw rugs on a green carpet. In reality they are gooey, slick, child worn patches containing nothing but clay.

"I've been missing you for coffee," she mentions while holding up her sophisticated Gevalia slim line thermos as a comparison.

A quart size generic stainless steel variety often is carried by husky, beer-bellied, whiskered construction workers to their work site. Aartemann carries the husky brand.

"It's been a hectic start, hasn't it? Stop by my office if you get a break. I won't have a regular schedule for a couple of weeks yet. We can catch up over a cup."

"You got a new sucker on a line after dumping that poor soul last spring, you old heart smasher?" Aartemann responds in jest.

Humorous banter is the verbal form that over half of their communication with each other takes.

"Why you paint-stained curmudgeon!" Abby retorts crisply while he opens the school entry door for her.

He bows as low as he can go with his always aching

back. A wave, a gesture of entry is completed by using his stainless thermos full of Starbucks.

Abby is this elementary school's counselor. She was divorced before Aartemann knew her so the only last name he knows of is Sledford, which is her married name before the divorce. She kept it since her two boys born in the marriage have the name. She says it seems easier or at least did at the time ... for them. Abby (perhaps Abigail) Beatrice (after a grandmother) Sledford, but Aartemann calls her Abs in private. Everyone uses Mrs. Sledford in front of the students. The name Abs came either from her continual exercising enjoyment (none ever actually witnessed by him), or just a short version of her full name, or just a shortened way for Aartemann to say Abby—as if that name needs any shortening. Aartemann thinks he remembers shorter names. He is bad at remembering names.

ABS is her initials he'd noticed once on the thermos. It could also be Aartemann's unconscious revenge for so often being referred to as a curmudgeon. He looked the word up long ago to discover if he was being praised or ridiculed. She uses the name so sweetly and gently that he has never been sure to this day. It's just accepted as coming from a closest of friend. Abs is that.

cur mudge on (ker muj' on)
n. a miser, greedy after gain, covetous, a rustic peasant, country bumpkin of lowest rank, rough tempered man, an unfeeling uncivil selfish narrowminded art teacher, Mr. Aartemann-like, a cranky old coot artist, churlish not to be confused with churchish.

Abs is a picture of fitness for a lady of her age. Her years are a count that no one ever really seems to know. She definitely seems too young to have children out of school. Yet she's mature in mind and spirit beyond an age that she really must be. She dresses sharp; her clothes are plain with just a touch of accessories to express elegance, not gaudiness. She is a skilled and compassionate counselor. And she dates. She attracts men that Aartemann is sure are younger, but even as her friend he can never get all the facts about the suitors. So he just pesters her in their friendly jousting way. Occasionally he counsels the counselor, but only when directly asked. Mostly he listens over coffee, just like she does with him concerning his own private life situations. They are that comfortable and without a fault, confidential. They have a lot in common. They are just two adults and overlapping education careers. They, in each their own ways are growing employment-weary. They are so alike or compatible that their single disagreement seems to be over their personal preference of coffee brand name.

They part on the inside of the door. Abs goes her office direction and the cheerful, grinning curmudgeon in the by rote path to the art room.

"Maybe later, Abs," he mentions not even looking at her, "I don't even have student names in my grade book yet."

Even Aartemann can not remember the rest of the hurry-up morning. The fury raced until the period scheduled for the largest class of the school. It is a fourth grade group. Unfortunately he has not even had time to take a break and relieve himself of the day's first four cups of Starbucks.

"It is sometimes called the grid system of drawing," he continues as he moves into the demonstration portion of the lesson.

He has already given a lengthy opening of the lesson verbally. It includes some history and appreciation. To his delight the students' attention is still focused. He has not lost them even in the heat that is not helped a great deal by the floor fans blowing at the class from two opposite directions.

When Mr. Aartemann was a student, two score and more years ago, school did not start prior to Labor Day, avoiding much of this late summer heat. Buildings did not keep up with educational trends that recognize comfort-aided learning.

"The time has arrived to begin the exercise that will help you learn to draw using this technique."

He reassures the class knowing he still has a five to ten minute demonstration to accomplish on the chalkboard. Only then will they get the paper to pencil their own first attempt.

While he draws lines on the chalkboard at the front of the room he explains, "This is a piece of paper divided into nine squares. Again, the process is simply to treat each square as a separate but simple drawing. Draw only one square at a time. You'll get sick and tired of me repeating 'one square at a time' before we finish with this assignment."

He has presented this lesson many times over his career and knows exactly what to expect. In the end there will be some great drawing results.

"Here is what I will attempt to draw for you using this grid system or one square at a time process."

He picks up off the overhead projector—now serving as a lectern—a paper. It was laminated years ago for annual use and reuse. In the other hand he holds a roll of masking tape. A dramatic gesture toward the chalkboard is made so the taping up detail is not missed by anyone. He exaggerates the struggle of taping the example sheet to the board by holding it in place with his elbow. Simultaneously, brown tape pieces are torn using both hands.

"On this example drawing of a house, the red lines you can see are overlapped with a grid of black lines that make nine squares. Each square holds only a few of the marks that make the house drawing. I am going to begin by drawing only what is in the first square, the square at the top left corner."

He gestures again overdramatically, keeping the student's attention by way of the exaggerations of movement. He then holds up the white cardboard sheet secured from the impromptu lectern. This is only after dramatically placing the roll of masking tape on a stool located in front. The stool is intentionally staged out of arms reach of the taped house example now located on the chalkboard.

The white cardboard has a square hole cut in its center that exactly matches the size of the house grid squares. The identical size allows it to be used as a shield. It blocks out all vision of adjacent squares. Only visible is the isolated piece of the grid intended for the drawing attempt. Like all good showmen, he is careful that the students only see one side of the cardboard keeping hidden the backside. That would expose four pieces of magnetic tape.

Carefully, the shield of cardboard is located over the house grid so only the first square is visible. Mr. Aartemann reaches to the right for the tape to secure the shield in the same manner that the house example has been taped to the chalkboard.

"Ugh-gh-h-h!" is his sound of stretching and groaning in his impossible attempt to hold the cardboard against the chalkboard hung example and reach the tape all at one time.

He tries a second time. He tries a third time. All are theatrical exaggerations to point out his dilemma. Fortunately, this time, no student runs up front to his assistance. Some helpful student has done that occasionally in the past. That nearly ruins what is to come next.

"Ah!" and he points upward as a sign that an idea comes to mind.

Students watch, some open-mouthed and some snickering, as he begins to draw with yellow chalk something looking like two pieces of masking tape on the chalkboard and across the two corners of the white shield. Once done, he lifts his hands from the shield in unison demonstrating the sticking success of his chalk drawn tape. Slowly he turns to face students, with a broad smile on his face. On their faces are some grins. Some are gasps. Some puzzlement, or rolling eyes on yet others—dependent on his successful deception of each child.

"How did he do that?" one whispers the query.

With a miser's bit of hesitation allowing for the awe to only partially diminish, for those students experiencing awe, the instruction goes forth.

"Don't try that at home. Remember, I am a professional."

With that statement, and another pause for mirth, Aartemann begins again with the demonstration.

"That first corner square contains only a single line. The exact beginning is located at the midpoint of the square's right side. I'll locate that end with a dot. The other end of the solitary mark is additionally plotted at the base of the square. A straight line connects the two accurate spots. Presto! The first square is completed. Square number one is finished. Isn't that easy?" the teacher encourages.

The shield of cardboard is impossible to remove from the chalkboard, at least as demonstrated by the teacher's severe case of overacting. Chalk drawn tape is erased from the top two corners finally releasing the shield. The white shield is then easily moved to the next square to be attempted. The top right corner square of the house drawing is identified as next to be done.

This time, for the persuasion of the nonbelievers, a nail is drawn with chalk in the manner that tape was drawn for the first square. It is large and overlapping the shield just like Mr. Aartemann had done moments previously. Dramatic emphasis this time is in the form of a fist. Noisy hammering on the chalkboard at the location of the chalk drawn nail's head is an effort to drive in the nail and the illusion.

"There!" Aartemann expresses with much satisfaction.

His slow turn to face the student audience brings into his view more faces of doubt than belief. There are always those, even at the age of about ten, that want so desperately to believe in the truth of the teacher. Surely the teacher is honest, knows all, and can do anything. And to a wee handful, Mr. Aartemann is super art man. Through the years, the old art teacher grows more and fonder of seeing just how far he can push their faith in him.

Again the students are left with no verbal explanation of the visual phenomenon they have just witnessed. Some are bewildered still. Some roll their eyes over and over in a silent comment wondering what this teacher/clown will try next. Others are beginning to accept a trick but cannot comprehend the possible solution to the "how" in their mind. Students that do not want to be considered fooled now begin to offer verbal potentialities. One or two are correct but largely go unheard because the one square at a time instruction is continuing. Attention of the class is truly riveted on the events of the chalkboard regardless of the reality or preposterousness accepted.

Erasure of the nail and the shield adjustment to a lower corner is completed. It is done without any drawing this time. The shield is again placed carefully and dramatically. While the left hand holds it in place with the assistance of a total body lean into the board by the art teacher turned actor, the right hand is being slowly waved overhead of the action. Aartemann's short fat fingers are being spread as wide as physically possible.

"See? The chalk tape and chalk nail were not real. It was a trick. It was really magic. You've heard the words abrakazam, wallakazo, please and thank you? It works every time! Don't try this at home. Remember, I am a teaching professional."

He has taught this lesson so many times he can actually do it now without smiling or laughing.

The grid-drawing lesson continues without further magic explanation. The advancing lecture quickly hushes the groans and verbal disbelief coming from the vast majority of the class at this point.

The moment arrives to demonstrate the final corner square. He pulls the shield from the board explaining simultaneously that the next square will be done without a shield.

"This will require more concentration to do the one square at a time," he explains.

Mr. Aartemann off-handedly tosses the cardboard shield at the board. Again he picks up a piece of chalk to work on the drawing example. A gasp comes from a front row table.

"It's a magnet!" the child astonishes verbally.

"Sh-h!"

Aartemann signals one-on-one toward the impromptu speaker.

"Some at the other tables still think I'm magic."

Mr. Aartemann tries to look embarrassed that he has accidentally given away the secret of his magic. Most of the students just laugh and make sure they are verbalizing to others at their table that they knew of the magnets all along. But some did not. Some really did not. Some were tricked. Some are amazed right up until the toss discloses the magnetism.

This method he uses every time he presents the one square at a time lesson and it never fails to fool some. Once in a while he almost feels some guilt for the dishonesty when he sees a youngster still trying to believe in the magic. Students long to trust in the reality of the teacher's truth. It is quite remarkable the faith students want to put into a teacher's words even when their own intelligence and reason is telling them that they are being tricked.

Is it not wonderful that the teacher of the most high, the Lord himself, uses no tricks or deceit in the message He gives to us all? His words are truth. His words and meanings are not hidden from view. His teaching is not hocus-pocus or smoke and mirrors but the open honest truth presented in a very simple form for all to understand. In God's word we can accept and be able to trust.

The word of God was put into parables not to distort but to more clearly express the faithfulness and truth of grace for all to know. The Lord's truth is simple enough for a child to understand. His truth is fact and carries no conditions.

All have been given the choice of whether or not to believe. All that we are told and presented by the Lord God, Jesus Christ, and the Holy Spirit is the truth, the whole truth, and nothing but the truth.

The art teacher really does not express the religious lesson that races through his mind at that point. It is unsaid even though deep inside he wants to shout it to the now fully attentive students.

Students stared at Aartemann through the pause caused by his thoughts.

Abs steps into the doorway just as he is about to complete the last of the demonstration, peers over her half glass readers, and shakes her head at Aartemann, having heard the past couple of minute's presentation without being detected in the hallway.

"Yes, Mrs. Sledford?"

"Sorry to bother this magical lesson, but can I see Sarah for a minute here in the hall?"

"Sarah," Aartemann begins asking Sarah who sat on the far side of the room away from the door. "Do you want to visit with Mrs. Sledford or do you want to stay and watch the rest of the demonstration by the world famous Magical Art Man?"

Aartemann's eyes returns to Abs in the door while the class looks to Sarah for her answer. Abs is rapidly checking out the students, and seeing all their individual attentions directed away from her and toward Sarah, she sticks her tongue out at Aartemann. She quickly tucks it back in. Abs tilts her head to her sweet look of "please choose me." Sarah gets up and heads for the door without a word spoken. Aartemann lets his mouth drop open. In that expression his head follows Sarah all the way to the door. Mrs. Sledford smiles hugely. She lifts her chin. She puts her arm around the shoulders of the shorter student. She turns them in tandem toward the hall for privacy.

"Meanwhile, back to one square at a time ..." and thus speaking, the art instructor goes on to complete the presentation perfectly timed for the remaining minutes of art class.

Sarah returns just in time to line up for the class exit and Abs gives Aartemann a flirty eyebrow flitter. This causes Aartemann to reflect inside, *She's one of the few I will truly miss if I quit. Will I miss this? Will I miss others? Will I regret? Surely not but how will I know? Oh well, lunch and prep now, I'll work on the resignation letter. I'll ask Abs.*

Aartemann looks down the hall for the counselor. Too late, she is gone. He reaches with a left hand to the small of his back. He rubs its ache. He prepares for the afternoon classes.

Granny Smith will be lunch.

A Born Leader

Teachers deal with new students all the time. Aartemann's school is in a neighborhood that has a high population of families who move in and out of the district, often due to job changes or rental situations. Of course the beginning of the year is always a classroom full of new students to get to know. Kindergarten teachers never have a student's previous teacher to go to and check history with. So, every teacher has nearly a pair of dozen new faces to deal with in every year. Others get more. Lucky teachers in a very small school might get less. Teachers that rotate through students, such as music and art teachers, like Mr. Aartemann, do not have a homeroom core. There are new faces and returning students to get acquainted or reacquainted with constantly. The educational level where everyone is on the same plane is in the earliest group, kindergarten.

The first arrivals of the kindergarten class on this day provide a variety of personality and activity. Sometimes when a kinder has had an older sibling passing through the same school, a teacher can have an assumed idea, at least an inkling, of what the younger child will be like. For the others it just takes some time. At least those with no sibling conjure no surprises due to wrong guesses. Kinders are an ever-changing lot as well. One day's behavior can change suddenly and drastically, like spring weather in Indiana. A passive sprinkle of a child can return to art class as a tornado with a mile wide base. It is part of what makes the youngest so much fun. It is also why Aartemann has a near balding patch above and between the ears.

Unfortunately, and quite unfairly, for some kinders, a concerned parent, usually mother, will provide a wee list of warnings. Nothing eliminates all of the surprises. Mother warnings are notoriously inaccurate, like mother pride.

Edward is a new kindergarten boy in the morning class at the elementary. Aartemann is Edward's first art teacher. Edward is not his real name but Mr. Aartemann has lately been caught up in the battles of historical Scotland through novel reading and Edward was a name back long ago that often went with royalty and take charge kind of nobility. So until he learns the students' names he is calling all of them Edward if they are male and Elizabeth if they are female. He even is considering renaming the school to Sterling Elementary after another great battle in Scotland. Some days the battle still rages on at Sterling.

Edward, no doubt, considers himself a born leader among peers. Perhaps it is attributed to the fact that he has a grandfather and an aunt that teach locally in the elementary system. That is not always a plus. Resulting from family pride and teacher habit, it appears they encourage Edward with every achievement. His every step is likely met with positive encouragement and with flowing accolades of leadership characteristics. Perhaps Edward's destined to be the next teacher in the family.

True leaders move quickly in any situation, and begin their role of organization and direction. That even happens in the youngest of elementary classrooms. Some even require to be taught that they, as a student, are under the authority of the teacher. Some kindergarteners battle hard at that thought. Most small students bow readily in fear or, more likely, in awe. Leadership among the peer group of students is up for grabs. Similarly it happens on a Scottish battlefield as the commanders who actually lead the charge, fall to mortal wounds. Only the strongest and only the bravest dare vie for the honor of "student supreme."

In an early week of the school year Edward's kindergarten teacher stepped out of her kindergarten classroom into the hall for a moment. She had something to discuss with another staff person and did not want the children to hear. She was however within visual contact and audio hearing of the room. Edward seized the day.

Edward simply, and in his mind quite honestly, announced, "Be good, kids. I'm in charge now!"

Edward's class will be the first to arrive on this school day. It will begin very soon and the art teacher has already placed needed materials on the tables for their project. It is the kindergarten preparation that gets him thinking about Edward and the other Edwards and all of the Elizabeths that soon would each have their own personality showing. Perhaps the art teacher will continue calling this one boy Edward forever.

"Best not," he thinks. "His grandpa will be calling."

He sits at the art room teacher's desk and props his legs on the right desk drawer of the old oak piece. The drawer is deep and intended for use as a file drawer. It is a perfect height for a foot stool. The chair he purchased with his own money several years ago to help his back pain swivels and tilts back, making it quite a relaxing position. A window just five feet to his left is opened and a screen defuses the slight breeze blowing in. It is a warm breeze, but not as warm as the day appears to be heading for. The art room is a corner room of the building with a basement prefix when talked about. Basement-art room! However the building's basement floor is only sunken into the ground about three feet, allowing for two full walls of windows and plenty of ventilation. The basement status makes it one of the coolest rooms in the building on hot outside temperature days. Only the principal's office and the school office, with air conditioning window units, are better. West facing classrooms sometime peak at over one hundred degrees on days like this day is pointing toward. Rank has its privileges always.

Aartemann watches students that live close by walk to the building. They pass through the playground and parking lot. He sees them pass his windows in pairs and trios. Occasionally a face will press against the glass trying to avoid the reflections and glare, spot him watching, and wave a hello. He waves back, or salutes. Most have a bag being dragged over the pavement. Others, more affluent perhaps, sport a backpack with a variety of colors, designs, and super action figures.

A very small child, probably an Elizabeth, falls but is helped up by an older student almost immediately. She gets her knees brushed off once she is standing.

"I wonder if that is a brother?" he ponders.

Aartemann continues watching the caring assistance take place in front of his eyes.

It will be another warm day in an unconditioned building. Most of the students are arriving with smiles. A few are hiding any kind of expression, blank. It makes him wonder about their home life. It is unknown what situation they leave behind. Little can be done to change what is ugly.

"Lord, let this warm day at least be pleasant with joyful spots. Give them a place in the day for a belly laugh. Warm each with Your presence, even those that yet do not know of You. Give me the ability to be cool and pleasing to each of those I encounter. Let Your presence pass through me. Let me help pass Your joy to their day. Let each individual student feel love from You, directly and through me and other Christian teachers, and one day, Lord, give each child the awareness that the love is of You. Help us as this school's staff fill up their minds with more than just facts. Allow Your Spirit to radiate throughout school today making the warmth and the breezes a sign of You. Amen."

With that quiet prayer, Aartemann drops his feet the height of the desk file drawer to the floor. The hard cement floor will hold his shoes constantly for the remainder of the day with perhaps the welcome exception of a fifteen minute rest to eat the apple. It is another large, green Granny Smith. He has carried it for his lunch. If he forgets he will eat it tomorrow. Some days he will forget his mini lunch treat due to the busy schedule and work through lunch on project materials preparation or hanging displays. He gets little time for that in this year's schedule. It is just like last year's. His belt holes demonstrate no serious problem with missing a few lunch apples.

Morning classes come and go. The kinders do not get the tables cleaned before the next class. A fourth grade group arrives at the door unescorted and a bit noisy. These two classes have no gap between the first class period's end the following's beginning. That near overlap unfortunately occurs several places in the weekly schedule. Classroom teachers who try to fudge an extra three or four minutes of released time into their schedule by sending pupils unescorted to special classes like art create the traffic jam. Today it causes a three-kindergartener pileup at the door. It ends with only bumps and dents, no fatalities.

Mr. Aartemann does not often present himself for idleness in the teacher's lounge. Here it doubles as a separate dining area for adults. Many staff uses it for lunch to get a rest from the noise and activity of students. He does not because he often, usually in fact, needs the time for the preparation, especially for this afternoon schedule, again with some back-to-back sections. He, today, has thirty minutes to eat and prepare for an additional four classes coming in the afternoon.

Aartemann discovered much earlier in his teaching career, at another school position, that he did not enjoy much of the lounge conversation. Often, occasionally perhaps in reality but much too often for his likes, talk became facts and stories of students that were unnecessary, cruel jest, or something that should have been privileged information.

He has never told many that is the primary reason for his lounge absence. That seems too much like preaching. He certainly considers himself no preacher. He knows the backlash of gossip. He's felt the hurt when it was not even involving himself. But he believes also one of the best ways to avoid it is simply to avoid places it frequents.

He talks with his wife about it.

"I'm no saint, nor guiltless, but in Proverbs 26:22 when it says 'The words of a gossip are like choice morsels; they go down to a man's inmost parts' it does not go on down with positive results. No it mentions then 'an evil heart' and a 'heart ... harboring deceit' and 'malice' in following verses."

She follows with, "Also in James 3:26, 'If anyone is never at fault in what he says, he is a perfect man, able to keep his whole body in check.'"

"I'm not perfect but less at fault if I am about my business—in my room."

Actually another reason, a very good one, is the fact that Mr. Aartemann is a Mr. The vast majority of elementary teachers, support staff, and even administration are Ms., or Miss, or Mrs., or whatever confusing politically correct prefix is currently fashionable. Being few males in a predominant woman's area makes for lunch discussion nothing at all like a male pool hall atmosphere. While not desirable to him, it does sound a better alternative than the female filled teacher's lounge. Well, at least when it is crowded. The once escape location of the boiler room, the male haunt of the elementary building, is much too foggy in this supposed smoke free environment. Besides, for the last five years now that is often occupied by the frequently used substitute custodian—Ms Mopp. (ed. Note: That is not fiction.)

Then why is he suddenly finding himself at the food table in the teacher's lounge? He is seated quietly, largely, but absorbent of the conversation. Half is that type of conversation he chooses to avoid interacting with. The second portion is the talk grandparents are made of.

He listens a great deal more than he speaks in such situations, this time is no exception. He inflicts upon the predominately grandparent age staff assembly (at least at this particular moment) his own antidotes of grandsons. He adds to the lists of what is hot and what is old stuff to gran's as well as the nostalgic list of what was when he and they were the grandkids.

Although the conversation remains about children it turns from students and conferences to family of the staff. It is politically correct in topic.

It was the smell of food that also drew him to the lounge. Today's aroma producing room is located less than ten steps from the art room doorway. It is the variety of bagged salty chips that draws him rather than the larger assortment of cake, cookies, candy, and other sweets.

He mixes a paper plate full of Doritos and Ruffles and is now alternating his bites when he becomes conscious. He grows attentive to a third grade teacher's tale of a young female family member, apparently a niece (not her own child). It is obvious, to her dismay, that the child and her family do not attend church. They have little occasion with religion of any persuasion. Thus the female child has no historical background of Biblical references.

It was the niece's desire to stay up late to watch a TV presentation lengthy enough that it ended beyond a normal bedtime hour. With some apparent coaxing and pleading the parents gave in to the child to allow the viewing of the movie *Moses*, according to the story being told by the teacher. Now there is a fully attentive lounge crowd.

She never shared, or Aartemann never picked up on,

whether the parents were watching the film while the telecast was in progress. The result of this story did assure that at least one of the adults was in the same room. And according to the teacher-storyteller it became apparent that none in the household knew of the story of Moses prior to this particular night of the telecast.

It must have been a masterfully done film to keep the attention of the younger family member. It was an event toward the end of the film's story that caused the anecdote to be retold to those gathered for their quick lunch in the teacher's lounge.

The child must have watched in awe the life of Moses, his being found and then raised in a different home. The events of his adulthood were strange and different to the child watching who had no prior experience of the life and stories of this Biblical character from the Old Testament.

To the child, the miracles and God interventions through the life of Moses had to look strange, fictional to say the least. Much was chalked up probably to special effects wonders of a talented film crew.

Finally the point in the story came alive on film where Moses, in his leadership role grasped his staff, raised it to God—as were his instructions—and of course the deep waters of the Red Sea separated to dry travelable land for the people to escape and enter into the Promised Land.

"Raise your staff and stretch out your hand over the sea to divide the water so that the Israelites can go through the sea on dry land," the Bible quotes in Exodus 14:16— words never heard by this girl.

Nor did she know that in Exodus 14: 21–22 it reads,

"Then Moses stretched out his hand over the sea, and all that night the Lord drove the sea back with a strong east wind and turned it into dry land. The waters were divided, and the Israelites went through the sea on dry ground, with a wall of water on their right and on their left."

According to the report from the taleteller, unknown to Aartemann since he did not watch the program because he has no cable TV or antenna, the televised movie showed the miracle as it took place just as recorded in the holy Word. In the movie, the waters were parted. At that moment the young un-churched niece stood throwing her arms into the air over her head and exclaimed, "Oh yah, right! Like that could ever happen!"

The teacher-storyteller finishes by explaining that with the sudden spoken unbelief, she, the niece, turned herself in the direction of her bedroom. She had enough.

Aartemann wonders and muses aloud if the girl exclaimed anything like that after seeing *Star Wars* for the first time. And he will think much afterwards of the story and the girl and of her unbelief. Would she ever believe? Would she ever hear more of the miracles of God? Would she ever experience God? Would her soul ever be saved as those Israelites? *It is a good thing*, he thought to himself, *that everyone in the lounge at the present time were believers, openly so, and probably believed the Moses story, and had done so most of their life.*

"And when the Israelites saw the great power the Lord displayed against the Egyptians, the people feared the Lord and put their trust in Him and in Moses His ser-vant," is another passage from Exodus, chapter 14, verse

31 that Aartemann looks up in his Bible he keeps on top his desk when he returns to the art room just five minutes prior to the first afternoon group, lips salty and breath smelling of Doritos.

"It's a good thing Moses didn't react like Edward," the art teacher chuckles and speaks to himself. "I can just picture Moses standing on a huge rock, staff raised and shouting, 'Be good kids! Be good children of Israel. I'm in charge now!' That has a much different Biblical ring to it, don't ya think?"

The art teacher decides to get moving since the next class comes soon.

Aartemann goes out of his way to check his office mailbox and retrieves his pay stub. The funds are electronically deposited. He passes by Abby's counselor office and peeked in since the door is cracked. She is at the computer and the room is otherwise empty.

"Can I have a session?" he asks her.

"I'd empty my schedule for you, come in. I was just checking on the progress of a bid on some coffee. Ebay you know."

"That stuff you bid on is not coffee. If you ever want real coffee, let me know and I'll give you the web site where I buy my Starbucks at discount and in bulk. Real coffee for a real man."

Aartemann holds up his stainless mug like offering a toast.

"I'm not a man."

"Ah, so right! Next thing we know you'll use Ms. in place of your Mrs.," he replies in a comfortably friendly jest as he eyes her and sizes her from head to toe several times and then sips his coffee mug. "Nothing meant there, sorry, but you'll never get that changed without a real man's cup of coffee every hour or so. And what are you doing, putting cane and cow into that stuff you do drink? Oh never mind, I see you drink a bit of coffee flavor with your milk. When it comes to coffee, Abby, you are a loser."

"You old curmudgeon!" she retaliates from habit.

"Got check-will doctor!" he expresses taking a seat in the softest chair he could find, skipping three folding chairs, and landing on his pockets with a bit of a groan. "The check has the raise on it finally, but the increase in the deductible on the insurance leaves me in the hole about three fold."

Abby nods her head in apparent agreement. "How's the back? Doesn't look too good from that attempt to sit. You taking anything? Have you seen a doctor yet? You've been complaining about that for some time now, you know? Aren't you supposed to know better?"

"Say something in counselor talk; you're beginning to sound like my mother. Uh, no better, no worse. Nothing!

No not yet, and what else did you ask? Never mind, I need your help. I'd get down on my knees to beg but I can't and that's why I need your help. Can you cover the last ten minutes of my last class today so I can leave in time to make a chiropractor appointment? Please? Pretty please, I'll bring you some real man's coffee?"

"Sure, uh ..." she looks at a schedule chart on the wall, "about 2:50 P.M.?"

"Thanks, you're a peach."

"And you're a curmudgeon. I told you I'd do that last week if you'd go see a doctor."

"Well I called this morning after dropping to my knees from a pain beside a student. I don't think they noticed. I just can't take the leaning over the desks. Maybe I need a wheel chair to move from one student to another. Wouldn't that look swell? Maybe I'm just getting too old. Maybe I'm already too old for this work. I think the chiropractor wants me to come in every other week at least for the next couple of months and then get back on a routine visit. Do you think I'm too old?"

Aartemann pauses and stares into his coffee mug and hears no answer from the counselor who is wise enough to realize the rhetorical questions were not directed at her.

"Seriously, Abby, you know me better than anyone here. With my health problems and ability do you think I'm getting too old? How do you know when it is time to quit?"

"You still a praying man?" she asks from her swivel chair.

"Yes, of course."

"You'll know."

"Oh thank you, give-no-answer counselor. Maybe I can go on forever since they put wheels on walkers now. Changing the subject, how's what's his name, you know, that guy you've been eBaying?"

"You curmudgeon. I'm not eBaying, but I might if I could. We're writing and calling. A lot! I wish he lived closer. As a matter of fact I have a couple of tickets to the program at the Holiday Theater Building. My favorite singer is to be there soon and I bought two tickets to take a friend. Problem is, I don't know anyone I'd rather take than him. Well you of course, but there's your wife. It's in the middle of the week and he's too far away to drive that long for one night. Would you and your wife like to have them? I don't think I'll go by myself or with anyone now."

"Ask him."

"Right!"

"No really, I mean it. Ask him and then fly him into Indy. He could be in from up north—Wisconsin isn't it?—and you pick him up, take a day off for mental health, go to the concert, and get him back to the plane in almost less than a day. He'll only miss a day of work. Isn't he the boss in that little firm anyhow? You know, lots of people do short hops on a plane like that in a day all the time. You got a raise. Isn't he worth it? What ya savin' all that money for anyhow? Don't tell me you'll spend it on that stuff you call coffee?"

"Now you're sounding like my father."

"I'm old enough. It's a senior privilege on the back of my AARP card." Aartemann watched Abby contemplating the prospect.

Her improving mood is demonstrated by signs on the corners of her mouth.

"Ask him, do it and then ask him, he'll come. It's okay!"

She smiled.

"Oh, I'm late. My next class is probably already there. Don't forget my class. I'll see you before three."

He jumps to his feet. He groans. He slowly straightens his back and with long strides is away in an Aartemann hurry.

Suddenly he is there again and startles her.

"I forgot to tell you, I'm looking at consequences of working just part time, job sharing the art assignment. I need to know what it will do financially before I ask about the possibility. I'll talk to you about it later. Top secret! Sh-h! No one knows but my wife and me; well, now you. Gonna need your help on this. Later!"

He is again off as spry and quick as Santa to the chimney.

E-mail Traffic

It may be the fasting since last evening's meal or the lack of the first cups of coffee in the morning, or the fact that it takes two tries before the nurse gets a vein to collect the blood for the blood test. Whatever the cause, Aartemann arrives at school a bit depressed and leaning more toward making this the/his final school year. Nearly every day he considers the question. Retire or delay? There is so much to consider when making a retirement decision and it has to do with more than money and insurance and health. He's no different than any other person in any other profession. It is a scary move that cannot be reversed completely once the retire decision is signed for.

Maybe it is the cloudy sunless sky that pulls him toward teaching escape. Maybe it is just the joy from remembering being at home the prior weekend with nothing demanding. It is a long drive today from the doctor's early office visit to the school. Because he is the first to get stuck by the lab nurse, Aartemann is in his classroom ninety minutes early. Normally he arrives an hour early. He pours a coffee, finally, from the thermos. He boots up the computer. He ignores the thirteen unopened emails. He mouse clicks on new mail to compose.

angail@skybase.ad

Some days in the life of a teacher, probably no different than any other profession, the work is not desired or even looked forward to going toward.

Other days there are moments that can make your day. Some days, like any other field; because I have felt it leaving to build a house and a day heading out to sell an advertisement ... but once in a while a teacher just wants to forget there is a class waiting and needing direction. Today is that day.

It is not because the job, the employment, is unwanted or non-rewarding, or distasteful, or any negative feeling at all. It is because there is an alternative, that cannot be an alternative really, that draws me even more than educating a young child. I am drawn this day to you, my wife, to a relationship, to love and togetherness that again I know without a doubt is above anything else in my life. All else, including an employment position, is second fiddle. It is but out of commitment and integrity that I am able to drive to the destination of teaching leaving behind the desire of companionship for this day.

I realized just this morning that our little prairie patch lot is more than just an acre or so of ground and water, wood and plaster. It is an attitude that has developed from living in that place and the relationship fostered in the blessed presence of Christ in every animal, leaf, ripple, chair, book, movie, olive, candle, and kiss. Our home is the combination of spirituality, marriage, fantasy, nature and the supernatural of all of the combinations as well as the blessedness of all those things combined in near perfect union.

Did I tell you I love you? Do you know you are

my home? Do you know you are the very breath of my life, a new life? Rest and wait for me, for this day with the wee ones cannot be long and then this day's truest desire can be completed. Thank you for being the angel of our acre. Did I tell you I love you? Foreverly!?

—A

The teacher sends his email note to his wife hoping she'll read it sometime during the day. He begins looking at the thirteen unopened messages in front of him. He recognizes her address. She beat him to the computer today.

aartemann@elementary.www

Hi, and good morning, Irish teacher warrior. Hope the blood work went okay, and the drive to school as well. Just wanted to remind you how much I love you, just in case you forgot. I'm sorry last night didn't go like I thought it might. I wish my fatigue and headaches would disappear, and that one day, I would wake up and feel perfectly "normal."

Been praying about your "pipe dream," as you called it, and I don't think it's a pipe dream, at all. I think we should pursue it, until there's a definite block in the road. By block, I mean, a true impossibility, not just a difficulty. How else will we know?

Let me know you've gotten to school on time, when you have a minute? Did I tell you I love you? I do, oh, I do. Even when this old body betrays us, I still do.

—G

Aartemann fired another email back in reply wondering if she was yet logged on.

angail@skybase.ad

Oh, I love you too! They just announced breakfast in the library this morning. Oh well, I forgot, besides my roll with cheese was still warm as I ate it leaving the doctor's office, and the coffee was hot, and what could be better because my babe made it special for me. She touched it!

The blood test was a two sticker, but I know you prayed. I hate it when they have to poke again. It seems to make them angry that they couldn't get my roller-coaster vein and they move on to the barbed needles and use the Captain Hook approach. At least they haven't tried leaches yet. It may not be too long and they'll be saying, "At your age forget the blood tests, it doesn't matter what your cholesterol is any longer."

Last night was good for me. Any time with you, even eBaying for your books, is wonderful. Yes, I too remembered a lingering kiss from the morning that I wanted to do further research on but ... I know I'm a bit wound up about the "Pie," you know, that "pie-in-the-sky" idea that seems to be browning nicely, the aroma is wafting, and nowhere yet in the tender flaky crust has it burst and bled to the oven floor to burn. And the Bishop, just this morning, preached at Father Tim's church (you know the Jan Karon audio book you picked for my truck driving) in an announcement that the Father and the Mrs. were setting off to Canaan. And I looked up, well I was looking while driving, I mean I was suddenly aware, and looked heavenward. It was like a sign from up above.

I looked it up in Genesis 12 this morning. This is "slightly" abridged and irreverently paraphrased.

The Lord had said to Aartemann, "Leave your country, your people and your teacher's desk, and go to the land I will show you. 2 "I will make you into a great nation and I will bless you; I will make your name great, and you will be a blessing. 3 I will bless those who bless you, and whoever curses you I will curse; and all peoples on earth will be blessed through you." 4 So Aartemann left, as the Lord had told him; and his babe went with him. Abram like Aartemann of the future was fifty-five years old when he set out from Haran. 5 He took his wife, his journals, all the possessions they had accumulated (golf clubs, reels, books, pizza cutter, tea cup and coffee mug, and a pair of folding patio chairs) and the retirement they had acquired in Haran, and they set out for the land of Canaan, and they arrived there.

Okay, Biblically scarred, but its close! Is it an omen? A sign!?

I sure did listen to the short sermon well, hearing that Abraham, Tim, and myself all did or would experience fear of the unknown, anxiety over a new direction, but also go with the promise of good things from the Lord Himself. A Biblical Omen?

Well, I best get to work. The kids enter the building in fifteen minutes and I've done nothing to prepare for today and I have not even taken a second cup from the hot thermos my sweets sent with me. Oh my dear, I wish to drive you to Canaan, and find milk and honey, and no head stuff. Did I tell you I love you?

—A

Morning classes pass with few hitches other than a slow arrival of the custodian to clean up a fluid spill from a sick student who sits at the blue table. Good thing it is a smaller class and an alternative table is available to move to quickly. The windows nearby help with the aroma, and it is mostly liquid void of chunks for the kids to talk about, and it is light of volume, and Bill, the custodian, is not really slow, it just seems so when an up-chuck happens in the art room. All three custodians in the building are of the name Bill. Bill C., Bill N., and Bill E., but he doesn't like to be called Bill E. It sounds to him like we are calling him Billy so he is just Bill. Bill cleans the spill.

What kind of administrator would hire three custodians with the same name?-Aartemann always thinks when addressing any of the trio. One day he will slip up and blurt out the question right in front of the principal and then his retirement question will be answered for him.

Someone like me that forgets names, is his always answered thought.

No projects are vomit hit or ruined. It takes a dedicated and battle worn art teacher to have concern over the art in the middle of a barf.

"Good bit of luck that happened prior to lunch. With a full belly it could have been a lot more," Aartemann mumbles loud enough that the yellow table and the red table hear his words.

Most snicker and others say "Gross."

angail@skybase.ad

Morning classes are past, third grade "snowpeople" (the weird snowmen project) are displayed in the hall, other grading and hanging loom, lunch time is here, and I'm thinking of you again. How did it go with your doctor visit? Did he have any suggestion as to the headaches of late? New meds or continue with the same old same old?

I love you and the work/semi-retire/retire question plus your health seem to be the only thorns in this "long stemmed rose" life that I so love spending with you. I shared with the school counselor a bit after she asked about you. She reminded me that life was not always perfect and as a matter of fact it never is and there is always a bit of this or that to deal with. I guess I need to remember that and also remind you, especially when it is my life changes that are raising the dust. Like you are dealing with your headaches by remembering in prayer those that are dealing with the pain of cancer, and facial surgery, etc.; I or we need to deal with some of our things as a bump in the road, a dust storm, that will pass, and remember that He is in our pains and that we have already recovered, no—more than that, we have received newness. NOBODY can know what we share, what we have just shared the past couple of days, what we will experience in the next tomorrow. I, we, need to fight getting down over dust, when the big picture of our life is so wonderfully "foreverly" fantastic.

Do you remember writing "foreverly" the first time? I love stealing words from you.

So as far as the weekend, that's a couple of days away and will largely depend on your headaches. We can order a room at 5:00 P.M. and arrive at 7:00 P.M. We can decide on the spur of the moment, make a call and have a room waiting for a get away weekend. We could on the spur of the moment, eat at the steak place, or do Chinese at that great place, then buy a new skillet, and fry heart shaped hamburgers in it the next day at home.

I hope my rambling, which is my counseling session today, is not discouraging but encouraging for you. I am missing you and wish I had not left you with the added mailing task this morning in such a rush. I pray that the book sale was a delight, not an anxious venture. I pray you will have headaches small if they have to be at all. I pray you feel deep inside you the love I have for you. I pray that I can be all that you need to keep your faith strong, your heart rich, your stress level low, passion high, and life full—full of tasty new recipes that require no measuring and preparation. I'd really like to share a slice of cheesecake with you. Did I tell you I love you?

—A

aartemann@elementary.www

Hi sweetie: I have been home only a few minutes. I grabbed a sandwich before coming to the computer and finding your messages. Of course I am in tears as I read your "counseling session," but I find it washes over me with great waves of love. Please rest assured; I do feel your love for me, deeply, without question. I know you will almost be home before you read this, but in case you read it before you leave; maybe it can ease your anxiety a bit. We will talk about my time at the doctor's office when you get here. Please pray for Doc's daughter's twins. The mama has been in and out of the hospital three times since last week, with contractions. She is only at twenty-six weeks, much too early for the twins to be born safely. They've now put her on bed rest, and probably she won't be able to go back to work. He was very anxious when I first arrived for my appointment with him and couldn't get her on the phone; the line was busy. So, about mid-way into the exam, I told him to go ahead and try reaching her again, which he did, and that was when he found out where the mother to be was with it all. It is pretty cool when your doctor and his family are our friends. So ... please keep praying for those wee ones.

Headaches ... I still have them. They are less severe today, but still frequent. It is sort of like "contractions," only not regular ones. I got some books at the library on headaches, so I'm going to read up. I'll see you in just a little while and fill you in on things. I love you so very much. Please know that I know that you love me, okay?

—G

angail@skybase.ad

Classes are over and I should be getting ready to leave school, but I had thoughts for you and did not want to loose them so I'll e-mail them to you, knowing you likely will not read them till I get home, so then I can read them to you.

It is a pleasure to sit myself down for a session of writing for yet another attempt to verbalize in written words the love that spans our souls. It is an impossible task yet tried so very often with such delight, knowing full well it will end in failure, for the love that we have cannot be expressed in words already created. That is why you gave us "foreverly." It says forever from the soul. I love your words, I love the words you write and you find and then send on to me to make my workday more of a pleasure. Those notes zipped over the computer prepare me for the close of the day which can once again be spent with you, beside you, and more.

Of what I am very aware at this time in our relationship, it is a love that is formed from the core. That core is a spirit. It is the Holiest of Spirit, the Christ Spirit, within you, within me, and from that comes a love soft as mist floating like fog over the pond on a windless morning. As it moves it encircles our heart. We have but one heart now. Our old hearts were damaged and scarred and bruised and left filled with holes and emptiness. That Spirit transformed our hearts into a single strong pulsing alive heart that carries the strength of us both but dares not work without the beat of the other. So each thump-a-thump of that beating heart that fills our unity with the nuance of rebirth cannot be isolated as coming from one or the other but rather from a single source. I can always picture two strong yet soft muscle tissues pressed so tightly together that a point of connection cannot be detected. Chambers are pressed in such an embrace that when one beats it is the activation of the other sustaining life. It is as one mass of tissue, warm, wet with life's blood, untouchable by outward forces that try to crush it. It is in, and will foreverly remain in that embrace of living love.

It is in the flow traveling through that heart that the love then is carried throughout each of us into every nook and cranny. Every nerve has been touched by love and impatiently awaits another touch, another flow, and another brush with emotional intimacy that will never be matched by humankind. We have what has never been and never will be duplicated. We have our perfect love, born of a core of Christ, perfected through the Spirit, and sustained with your word, foreverly.

I will love you beyond our foreverly, lovely g. I will want for you always and totally until the one thing that can distract my desire for you is looking upon the face of the Lord that created us and joined us and taught us to love as completely as He loves us Himself. But we will yet be together, looking at Him, within the multitude of believers of heaven, no doubt finding a love that finally surpasses what we now feel for each other. In the meantime, and for this lifetime, know, I love you. I am leaving now. I will try to beat this e-mail home. Did *this* tell you I love you?

—A

They eat shaved turkey sandwiches and Doritos for supper. She has her tea and he, his coffee. She lays her medicated headache on his lap and he reads a George MacDonald novel. He holds the book in one hand and makes tiny circles on her temple and forehead with a finger of his empty left hand. They are together. They are silent. It is enough for this fine large day.

The Bedlr

Yancy Cain is somewhat of an unfortunate child, according to the art teacher's way of thinking. He believes it for no other reason than just being afflicted with the name of Yancy. Now Yancy in itself is not such a bad name. But it is uncommon. When other factors of a child in any elementary school are equally uncommon, it leaves something of a mark. It is a badge to be worn. Perhaps it is so of any name, Jack, Joe, Betty, Sue, Fred, John, Mandy, or any other common name as well. If a student displays any uncommon traits of behavior and intelligence; then the name they are christened with becomes descriptive. Thus Yancy is a Yancy. In mind, in ability, in manner, in scholarship, in appearance, and in sociality, Yancy is just that, Yancy. Yancy will never be a leader or overachiever.

The process of creating a pattern to use in the art class tessellation project is not a difficult level for most students. The students are given a bit of background about the Dutch artist, M. C. Escher, born in 1898 and living to 1972.

"That is the same birth and death years of my grandmother," the art teacher, Mr. Aartemann, shares with the class. "She didn't know anything about tessellations. She didn't even know M. C. Escher. But she was a fun grammaw."

Mr. Aartemann explains the mastery of Escher's art. It is a delightful type of art that shows the artist's success over the infinite and the impossible. Such is found in his drawings of four flights of stairs all descending and yet returning to the origin. Also he drew waterfalls spilling four drops but ending in the same initial pool of water. Aartemann uses an overhead transparency of *Drawing Hand.* It is a 1948 drawing showing one realistic looking hand drawing on a paper the image of a hand which in turn evolves into a three dimensional view of the hand rising from the paper into a hand drawing another hand, and around and around it goes. He uses reproductions of tessellations showing the limitless duplication of m.c.'s animal tessellations. They include bats, fish, birds, moths, and a lizard or alligator-appearing shape that "fills the page linking the tessellation pattern perfectly with no negative space, much like a jigsaw puzzle fits together."

He continues, "Although it seems impossible to create a shape that fits so perfectly to create such a design, it is rather simple. I'll demonstrate with this three inch square piece of tag board paper and then you will produce your own pattern for your own M. C. Escher-like art. I don't expect many of you will be able to produce a tessellation shape that is a recognizable animal, like Escher," here Mr. Aartemann pronounces the artist's name in a third different pronunciation, "but a non-objective tessellation is all that is required."

The majority of the class is able to produce five to ten of the potential patterns. Yancy creates three but out of the three, none is done completely correctly.

"Yancy, try using this same idea, do the cutting and taping again. Try a little more careful use of the scissors so nothing of the square of paper is cut off and lost. Then I will help you, if you want me to. I'll tape the pieces to the opposite side of the square to finish the pattern. It will be a fine shape and quite intricate. You can do it if you take your time."

And he does. Mr. Aartemann assists slightly with the masking tape to see that the cut pieces are exactly across the original square when reattached. The pattern is ready for the work of the repeated drawing around the heavy paper pattern. Those lines will create the tessellation outline on the twelve-inch square tag board paper Yancy has chosen for the finished piece. That will happen in the next class period since time is nearly over. He will eventually take that entire period as well as a second. It will take a restart on the back of the tag board to get Yancy's project ready for the color addition.

Aartemann sometimes nears tears with Yancy-like students. He's never exactly sure if he is sorry for their inability when their desire is keen or if he just gets frustrated with artistic deficiencies. God should have made it easy for every human being to create something beautiful. Such success would be able to solve a lot of social woes. The older he gets the more he talks like that to God and asks why all the difficulties down here on earth. Aartemann knows He listens. Aartemann smiles when he thinks about God listening to his suggestions for changes in His creation. God smiles too.

"Colors, textures, patterns, gradation, details, color tools to be chosen from markers, crayons, and or colored pencils will be your decision and should be based on all you have learned over the previous five years of art classes. Black and white is also okay since M. C. did that often himself." (Notice Mr. Aartemann steers from the use of the last name of which he has confessed he does not know the correct pronunciation.) "I do recommend that you limit the colors to two, three, or four colors. Also use variations like tints and shades—just as our featured master artist did in his own work. Above all else, whatever your choices, do it very neatly. Work carefully. Avoid the scribbled look unless it is a texture. But to be truthful, I do not recommend a scribbled texture."

Oh how Mr. Aartemann hates mentioning scribbling as a texture. Someone always thinks of it as a last minute, easy, sort of fill in that usually gets out of control. Then it destroys what starts out to be satisfactory. Taking time for craftsmanship is always a challenge with teaching elementary art students.

Yancy chooses colored pencils. He simply colors each of the shapes with a different color, with no pattern to the colors. No gradation or any continuity in the direction of colored pencil strokes is used. Although that was suggested to avoid a scribbled look, Yancy chooses the multiple directional less sophisticated techniques. It is easier and a bit quicker. Each of the shapes created from his original tag board pattern do have a predominate direction of texture caused by the strokes of the pencils, but each shape also has multiple direction strokes competing with the predominate ones. But one shape differs from the next, or does not, depending on the apparent whim of the ten-year- old artist at the moment of application of any particular pencil hue. One redeeming factor of Yancy's work is the fact that the intricate curving cuts he has completed when making the pattern ends with a tessellation shape that resembles a bird in flight. It has a wing span unlike an Eagle or a wren, or any particular bird. It has a tiny body more like a hummer than Canadian goose. It has a short scooped neck but nothing like a swan. It has a large head with a hole for an eye drawn. An eye detail is left only to the viewer's imagination. A pointed beak is protruding from the head, normal size for this bird's head, and split at the end resembling a beak detail most likely recommended by Aartemann. A flock of the outline shape flies toward a map directional west.

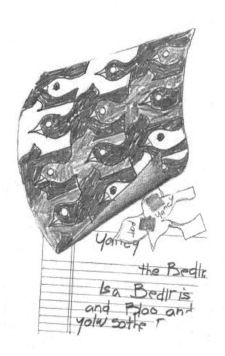

He, with Mr. Aartemann, eventually talks about the bird potential. Yancy even attempts a few sketches of possible details. Details could be added over his already finished coloring. The details prove somewhat less than satisfactory. Yancy moves on to the alternative of writing rather than adding foul fowl details. Any time students have remaining after all drawing potential is exhausted is to be spent writing a rough draft about the project. Most students spend the time, when available, telling how well they like doing the project. They write what they learned. They write why they chose the colors. They phrase something about the artist M. C., or why they are glad this project is about to end. Yancy is different. Yancy writes a fantasy story. He writes it in his own language. It is his attempt at good English writing. However, spelling, punctuation, sentence structure and anything else that is normally graded, is and always has been a difficult area for him.

When projects are picked up the final time, students who write about the project also turn in the written drafts. These will then be typed into the computer by the teacher and printed out for display along side any of the selected tessellations. It makes art displays much more interesting to read a bit of the struggle or decision making behind an elementary art project. And it is a way this school integrates one subject into another. It integrates writing skills into the related arts areas: visual art, music, and physical education.

Yancy is different. Yancy is different with what he writes. He cares not to describe how he completes the visual portion of the project. He has a story marching through his brain that comes from the outline of his tessellation pattern. He did his best to get it onto paper. It would be interesting to know if the visual or the written portion that Yancy turned in was the more difficult for him. Aartemann ponders which part he felt was most successful. He surely did not know that he has attempted something, by writing fantasy fiction, which no other student of Mr. Aartemann has ever tried. Again, Yancy is different, but in a positive way.

> the Bedlr.
>
> Is a Bedlr is color the is sky Re and Bloo and gren
> and yolw so the Bedlr is King of lan and is at in tree
> or fits eat and the Bedlr case cat wit fess and run tord
> dog and tord bull and kill and eat sum cat wit fess
> and cook cow wit a tree on fir and run aron the hos
> lot of 90 and fly in sky bloo and blak and ran stop
> fir the end

At first reading, Mr. Aartemann recalls a book he had been reading two days earlier when trying to come up with a new project for second grade students to honor the birthday celebration of Dr. Seuss. *One fish two fish red fish blue fish* was the title of the Dr. Seuss book that continued with

> Black fish blue fish old fish new fish. This one has a
> little star. This one has a little car. Say! What a lot of
> fish there are. Yes. Some are red. And some are blue.
> Some are old. And some are new. Some are sad. And
> some are glad. And some are very, very bad. Why are
> they sad and glad and bad? I do not know. Go ask

your dad. Some are thin. And some are fat. The fat
one has a yellow hat. From there to here, from here
to there, funny things are everywhere.

And on and on the book goes with fifty-three more pages
rambling from one animal to imaginary things with never
a fish to appear again. That style of rambling and writing
made Dr. Seuss very famous.

Was Yancy another Dr. Seuss in the making? He also
resembles other authors filled with imagination and not
letting ways of nature and this world dictate what could
be in the stories world. J. M. Barrie did it with Neverland
and Peter Pan—shadows and flying and fairies and never
growing up. George MacDonald wrote like that with a trip
on the back of the north wind as well as other fantasies,
which made him famous in his own time. Disney built
his own little world around such things that can never
truly happen. Is Yancy making up characters, and words,
and fantasy, or is this just a struggling elementary student
unable to express his story in picture or words correctly?

Mr. Aartemann seeks out Yancy's homeroom teacher
and eventually, through the help of a resource teacher, the
true story in Yancy's head is placed into a language that
we all can enjoy. The fact that he is asked to rewrite his
story, that it is being appreciated, that more is wanted, and
that it likely will be displayed is absolutely huge to him. It
is perhaps his crowning achievement to date. Yancy rib-
bons are few.

"Go ahead and add anything extra that Yancy desires
to his story. I love it so far and more would be great," the
teacher is directed by Mr. Aartemann.

Once the writing and word processing of the story is done a printed copy is completed. The assisting teacher accompanies Yancy to the art room to deliver the rewrite in person. Yancy's pride is wider than the smile that seems to spread beyond the width of his face. This is indeed an achievement seldom with precedence. Yancy is having a grand day.

The art teacher has to wait to read the result since another class, kindergartners, needs his attention at the time. It will be at lunch before the paper, now grown to half a computer page in length, can be read by him. He discovers later that Yancy had wanted to fill the computer page with the story. Class time allocations encouraged a swifter close to the adventure. For a time, Yancy "rolled."

Being able to compare the original writing, which includes the misspelling so great that words were incomprehensible and sentence structure nonexistent, with the completed edited and updated version of the fantasy by young Yancy Cain, unfolds a glimpse into the struggles of communication for Yancy. Yet the story is a delight.

> The Bird
>
> It is a colorful bird (Bedlr in the original pencil draft)
> of red and sky blue and green and yellow. It spits lava
> and fire whenever it wants to. It can fly upside down.
> He uses his fire to scare lions and people from the
> house they live in. The bird chases after a cat and the
> bird spits fire on the tree the cat lives in. The cat has
> a fish in its mouth and spits it out in the fire. The tree
> is on fire and cooks the fish. The bird eats the fish.
> The people try to put out the fire. The tree burns and

the cat and the tree fall on the house. The house is on fire. The dog chases the cat. It is on fire. The people have a bull and it sees the cat and the dog and the bull chases the dog. The dog runs in the house. The bull chases the dog in the house. The house kills the bull. The dog runs out the door and chases the cat again. All of the people try to put the fire out. The blue sky is black and the rain puts out the fire. The cat catches another fish and the bird spits fire and cooks the fish and eats it. The cat catches 90 fish. The dog chases the cat and the colorful bird eats the fish. The bull does not live a long and happy life. The end.

The art teacher enjoys this new fantasy author, as he has already enjoyed MacDonald and Barrie. He delights to such a degree over this short story that he copies the page in order to take it home and share it with his wife, also a lover of books.

The close of this tale will have to be the fantasy of its readers. Will the imagination of Yancy carry him into adulthood? Will writing provide a portion of his living? Will Yancy learn to succeed in any normal way? Or is he too different? Will his life end happily ever after or will he mime the bull and "*Not* live a long and happy life?"

You decide, but remember, Yancy Cain is different.

A Very Young Art Room Visitor

This day begins simply enough. It has the makings of a very long, an unusually extra long day of employment. Today is on the list of days just to be tolerated. He must put in the required hours like all the other teachers on this longer day. The dreaded length is dedicated to an afternoon and evening of parent-teacher-student conferences. He has no scheduled conferences but he is to be available for impromptu conferencing if parents would like to talk to him about their child's aesthetic education. He will have few, perhaps none. Most of the parents do not even know what aesthetic education is. He would not know himself if he had not been an art education student in college a couple of generations ago.

It should be a rather easy and stress free day with the exception of its length. The afternoon and evening will be used for catching up on displays and project preparations. Of course most of the projects ready for display are already hanging in the hallway art gallery. He calls the hall his gallery. Sometimes he sees the basement location of his room more like a tall ship's galley. Regardless, he displays art in the gallery in case a parent takes the effort to descend to the basement and the art room.

He is again contemplating his struggle over his employment. Retirement? His new off-the-wall idea is of a shared position putting him into semi-retirement status. The conference day and its free time may be spent later composing a pair of letters for potential use. One letter will be readied for the early retirement request. Retirement advance notification must be submitted by a contracted date to be eligible for early retirement financial benefits. The other will be a query into the possibility of a job shared art assignment for the next year and beyond. His decision is not made. In reality, Aartemann is still harboring a quite confused state. Perhaps the composing of the two letters will help in the decision making. At least they will be ready when a decision is finally come.

But this day is just beginning. The 5:45 A.M alarm programmed for radio broadcasting slowly alerts him. Normal awakening time signals the beginning of the long day to be spent at the schoolhouse. It unfortunately will follow a not so restful night. He awakes to do a roll, a cough, and a blanket (actually a sheet since he is plenty warm) adjustment. The normal routine of a thirty-minute crawl from the bed is shortened due to the necessity of getting to work just a bit earlier than normal. He is to join a meeting of the United Way Fundraising Committee of the school. The meeting is scheduled in the school library at the 8:10 A.M official start of a teacher's contracted work day. He had volunteered for the United Way drive committee at the school. Now on one of the longest days of the year, at 5:46 A.M, he wonders why.

The school day will be cut in half for the students. Many of them will return in the evening, however, with parents, or a parent, for their conference. Buses arrive at the earlier dismissal time at the school, load them up, and return them home shortly after noon. The remainder of the school day and long into the evening will be devoted to conferences. Thus the actual end of the teacher's day will prove to be near 8:00 P.M. followed by a half hour plus drive home for Mr. Aartemann.

The entire time, by the clock, for employment consideration totals nearly fifteen hours for a day like today. It will happen four times this year. It moves slowly for him since almost no student or parent chooses to visit the art teacher. A conference with him is not required nor recorded.

His day then is filled at school with four classes in the morning followed by plenty of time to do whatever. He will grade. He'll mount a few just completed pictures. He has been given no schedule nor has he created one for himself as to the plan of events and tasks for the noon to 8:00 P.M. student-free time span.

This day, three of the four art classes will require no teaching lecture. Students are finishing existing assignments. These are what he will grade later in the day. Only one class requires his instruction. It is an easy half day of teaching. He makes sure at home that his soft-sided brief case includes a novel. It is a Christian novel by a Scottish preacher/author aged at least one hundred years. He likes those. He's an eBay junkie for old Scottish authors' books.

The fourth class of the morning, and also the last of this day, is a fifth grade level needing nothing from Mr. Aartemann but the distribution of their unfinished projects. It's a tessellation design in the style of M. C. Escher. A pair of students, the first two to enter the room, are given the stack of drawings to distribute and with no

needed comments, the students secure necessary drawing media from the counter beside the sink. Like well-
adjusted students they set themselves to work. It is a good
working class.

Sometimes when classes are going well and projects
are far enough along that little instruction is needed,
Mr. Aartemann can be heard to "think" (he'd never say it
aloud), *Wow, and to think, I get paid for this!*

He turns on a CD of Eden's Bridge, Celtic music, and
sits at his desk to put himself to work. Once again he pro-
gresses on a teacher made example of a new project, begun
with the third grade level just this week. Any project he
requires of his students, he also attempts himself using
exactly the same materials the students must use. It helps
him find areas that might be a problem for the children. If
he can't do it, he could never expect them to accomplish it.
And, they will need at least as much time as it takes him
to do the same assignment.

His mouth drops open as fast as his feet push his five-
wheeled chair across the cement floor toward the child. His
grandson who lives two and a half hours from this school
nearly jumps into his reaching arms. What a soul kissed
hug it is. What a surprise! Fog blurs grandpa's eyes.

He cannot remember an unexpected event as pleasant,
as joyful as this. His grandson's entry is followed immediately, at a ten-foot interval, by the boy's dad and mother.
She is carrying in her arms the second and younger grandson. Aartemann is almost sure, had the room not been
filled with fifth grade artists, he would have shed some
tears. He is close to doing it. Due to the conditions, and

his old inner spirit wishing to be in control always, he simply swallows hard three times and hugs away. He noticeably has the grin of the cat that swallowed the canary.

His grandson is pretty big for two. Off the scales the doctor says of his two year height and weight. The room being filled with working fifth graders and art things encourages his investigation. He immediately begins checking out all the things on the teacher's desk. Mr. Aartemann, grandpa, actually just "Pa" to this boy, grabs a blank piece of tag board paper and the colored metallic green pencil he had been using on his own project attempt. Pa pulls out a writing board from the desk's right side. The new arrival is off to work on his abstract creation. Pa beams and floats.

Just about as quickly he spots the computer. A tiny hand points to the screen. His dad, Aartemann's son, interprets that he wants to see the "clouds" on the screen saver image.

"They're just beautiful," the grandson says pointing and drawing out the word beautiful.

At the same time his father is checking out the teacher desk clutter and recognizes the wood saguaro cactus carving. The brown twelve inch sculpture he and his wife had gifted to Pa on a long ago Christmas. The carving is of a very hard and dark wood looking very southwestern or Mexican. It has a natural finish allowing the grain of the wood to follow the curves of the cactus arms. It serves as a family reminder, and also serves on a practical level as a masking tape roll holder. Smooth, thorn-free arms sport two rings of masking tape at any given time.

He, Aartemann the younger, sits at the desk. He's

taken over the abandoned upholstered teacher seat and is leaning back in the comfy chair. He watches the activity while his wife and the grandson settle into an empty space at a student work table. They enjoy some creative time together in the art room. Aartemann carries his younger grandson of ten months about the room answering the obvious questions.

"Is that your grandson?"

"What's his name?"

"Thor."

"No, really."

"Doesn't he look like a Thor? That's what his Uncle D calls him."

"How old is he?"

"I'm finished. Do I have to write about this project?"

"Of course."

"How much time do we have?"

"Is that your son?"

"No, it's some strangers that stole my grandchildren and came here to trade them for ransom. Can I sell your painting for money to pay them?"

"Yeah, right!"

"Is it time for you to go yet?"

This time it is Aartemann asking the male student.

The gran' Aartemann is carrying is interested in chewing on his photo ID. The card is a plastic charge card size image of him attached to his necktie. The baby is in the process of cutting through three more upper teeth to accompany his single upper tooth and four lower teeth. He is alert and very pleasant as he chews. He is depositing wet slobber spots beside food spots visible from another previous wearing of this particular tie. Mr. Aartemann is known school wide for his ties. Goofy, ugly ties—some with spots. His pink tie, just pink, gets the most reaction, but a black tie sporting a herd of fluorescent pink pigs takes a close second. Pink attracts attention when on a man in the elementary. Probably anywhere! Aartemann's conservative nature is not reflected in necktie choice.

Many of the ties were purchased on eBay. Cheap! No one else would bid or be caught dead in them. A friend also gave him a grocery bag of wild old-fashioned ties, wide ties—ties from an estate of an old man who died. Even the Goodwill and the local Bargain Basement Store didn't want them. Actually, although quite out of style with large designs, they were more normal than Aartemann's collection that includes Taz, several Bugs Bunny ties, M&Ms, Mr. Potato Head, several Santas for the holiday, the Eiffel tower, Mutant Ninja Turtles, a Monet, a Van Gogh, Cat in the Hat, fish with a Bible verse about going with the flow (or something like that, nobody reads it), a computer mouse (yes, a rodent), a large sunflower bought in Romania, an old-fashioned and dirty wide gray, orange, and brown thing bought in Skibbereen, Ireland, a Donegal Tweed hand woven tie from Donegal Town, in County Donegal, Ireland—old enough it now has a moth hole—Taz licking a Bugs Bunny stamp sold by the USPO, a Campbell's company tie decorated with soup cans and veggies, a black tie to trick people at school and to wear to funerals, many others similar, and two nice ties bought by the son and his wife now visiting in the art room. That son is embarrassed when he considers his dad, the art teacher, in public with pink pigs or Taz on his chest.

His son's family of four did not realize when they came for an anticipated five minute visit that Pa would be free of classes and responsibility just twenty minutes following their arrival. This freedom is due to the shortened school day for the conferencing. Therefore, they decide to stay through the fifth grade art class. Pa readily agrees to join them for lunch at some local fast-food supply. What a treat for Pa!

"McBurger has no playground here in this town. Let's try instead the Burger Blaster. I'll meet you there. It's right in front of the Goodwill Store and I need to check out something there anyhow. They had some baskets there cheap that could be used for a drawing assignment in fourth grade. Who knows, they might even have a usable necktie. It's my favorite men's accessory store."

His son shakes his head while finishing the strapping of the boys into their car seats.

Pa kisses the older gran' and promises, "I'll see you at the burger store and we'll share some French fries, okay?"

"Fense fies," he agrees, smiling huge.

The total visit lasts a bit beyond an hour from the art room surprise till the departure end at the Burger Blaster parking lot. It is such a wonderful hour that it makes the remaining hours of this long day pass faster than they would have under normal developments. It is a brief visit but packed with such joy that it will remain a good memory forever.

It's love! It's what a wee bit of love surprise can do. It can become a life memory. Love moments with a child, a spouse, a dear friend, and of course, God, can produce the same result.

If every teacher has a long conferencing day like he is having, any future conferences will be pleasantly looked forward to and joyously anticipated.

"Oh, come on in. I'm Mr. Aartemann, the art teacher. This is the art room. Its 4:00 P.M., and you are the first visitor this afternoon. Come in, look around, there are more projects hanging in the hall, take your time. If you have any questions I'll be right here. Oh, hi Dad, you're here too. Great! You are the first visitors to art."

They will also be the last parent visitors this afternoon and evening.

"Hi Abby, you still here? Can't you slip out without anyone noticing? Do you have to stay through till the end? Dumb question, of course you do. So, what's up? Oh, guess what, my son, his wife, and the grandsons visited just at lunch time and we went out together. What a delight. I wish I could kiss this job goodbye so I could spend lots more time with them and do more kissing of those boys before they're of an age they don't want that activity. What can I do? Sit down; let me fill you in on my latest idea. It's a bit wild, off the wall, a "never done it like that before" type of idea. Think this will fly?"

Aartemann spends a good time discussing the pros and cons of job sharing. They seem tonight mostly pros and Abby watches the excitement in his eyes. She is seeing that he is beginning to get the idea that his last year is under-way, at least a last full year of teaching. She shares with him before they turn out the lights and head home that she has purchased a round trip ticket from Chicago to Indy and back the next day. She has asked him after all. He is coming for the concert. Aartemann and Abby are probably the only two staff leaving for home after the 8:00 P.M. hour with smiles across their faces. Every other teacher only thinks of having to return in less than twelve hours.

Mr. Aartemann and his wife now have a tradition of beginning the decorating of their house for Christmas on the occasion of Halloween. October 31 means lights out on the porch. The night requires working in the back of the house on a tree that requires assembly. Four are tra-ditionally placed inside their home for the holiday. The stores have already begun the Christmas displays so the Aartemanns feel no guilt in beginning Christmas trees at home. They received an unsigned/unstamped letter in the mailbox a year earlier complaining of lazy people not taking decorations down immediately after the holiday season. The letter arrived in May, well prior to Easter. And it is only a couple of wreathes used outside.

"I've got an idea," he shares with his wife. "How about, turn on the porch light and when the little masked Halloween panhandlers arrive we can have them sit down on the steps and share a Bible story. When they say, 'Trick or treat,' we will say, 'Tale then treat,' and offer an apple treat during chapter three of the Bible story. I can just hear them spreading the word out on the street of the neighborhood. They'll tell every ghost, goblin, and costumed super hero to avoid our house. I can just see those high school kids that come to the door demanding candy without even masking or costuming, running for their very adolescent lives away from the Bible story. Okay, I didn't think it would work anyhow. Leave the porch lights off and hand me the long branches with the blue tips. I'll work on spreading the branches while you make the coffee. Use some of that Christmas Blend I picked up on eBay last month. Tomorrow night, if this tree is up, we can make the first batch of party mix. Oh, and g, Merry Christmas … and BOO!"

PyroArt

There was already one burn on the drawing paper laying flat against the student worktable. It was a scorch going from brown tones on the outside of the circle burn to a dark black in the center indicating it had been just seconds from actual flame. The diameter of the mark of heat was perhaps one and a half inches. It resembled the size of one of the older style silver dollars that ended with the Eisenhower dollar.

I used to get a silver dollar from a grandparent for birthdays. Or was it for Christmas? Was it from grandma or grandpa or both? I can't remember, I don't think. Does it matter? he would mumble inwardly with the thoughts bouncing off skull walls. Thought bits cruised between brain cells and other matter like it was running lost through the woods, bouncing off trunks and brush. It happens to him, at times. Often the thoughts have nothing to do with the present.

The student was just lifting his head from a near direct mouth contact with the drawing paper. Smoke followed his rising mouth in a spiral. It looked almost like the shape of a small tornado in white. Acrid swirls of smoke floated and drifted following weak air current caused by the child's head movement rather than the self-producing wind associated with a fire. It was not a mini firestorm. There was no flame. The smoke seemed to originate from the second burn still in a smoldering state eight inches from the other mark. They were equal in look and size but this second gave the impression of "hot" due to the smoke that rose and literally was still connected to the young child's mouth, leaving the source of the attempted combustion in little doubt.

Aartemann stood across the room. With his primary attention on the needs of a young girl, he had by happenstance caught the smoke-trailed lift of the boy's head movement. The results of what he had just witnessed out the corner of his eye should have caused much disbelief. At the least, shock. But instead his initial reaction was anger. Anger was near the level of rage. The change showed in his expression, causing the girl to half step in reverse. She was unaware of what had been seen. She was thinking the unpleasant expression of the art teacher was directed at something she had done. She didn't understand what. What had she done?

This was not the first of Aartemann's art students who had accomplished setting fire to a project. This was the first elementary child to try committing the arson in his classroom, and this was only a first grade student. Times have changed. The other experience, thankfully only one other, was when a high school art student covered a board which needed a texture with volatile rubber cement. Then he placed it in a sink basin and ignited it with his—the student's—cigarette lighter. Four-foot flames were instant, but short lived. And the student was smart enough to be at arm's length when lighting the fumes. Fortunately that experience happened in the days prior to schools having ceiling mounted fire sprinkling systems. The entire art room facility could have been a class cooperative water-color day.

He bolted across the room. Aartemann flew, passing the girl as a blur, and at a speed surprising even him. He did a left arm hold around the waist of the primary student he had already lifted right-handed. It was a sudden sweeping motion uncontested. The young boy did not even see him coming. He hung from his left elbow joint like a forty-pound sack of potatoes. Fireman/teacher Aartemann used his now empty right hand to retrieve the scorched white paper drawing. As the fluid motion continued out the art room door he never looked back to see if the smoke trail followed them. Failing to look, he had no idea how the remainder of the first grade class was sizing up the action.

A few witnessing students were shocked, staring and standing stock still as the art super hero whisked away the culprit.

Actually his nature is normally not that aggressive, sudden, or reactionary. This incident seemed to strike him like nothing else had over the past twenty years of teaching elementary art. He was instantly in a zero tolerance mood. He was simply appalled that this tiny first grader would have the nerve to attempt to set fire to his project on his work table using his breath. Times have changed.

It was quite a jaunt up the two flights of steps. Clomping feet then were heard down a pair of halls. Finally, the principal's office. In his nasty fit of revenge for the child's audacity he wanted discipline done—severe discipline—and he wanted it now. The child still hung limp, his jerky movement was only caused by Aartemann's own jarring, undignified gait in the office's direction.

Somehow he got the office door open even though both his hands clutched a share of the evidence. Heavy thick wood construction of the door had an upper half of glass as a window. Now he remembered exclaiming his demand angrily and loudly.

"I want this as evidence!" he had shouted as he snatched it up with the art student.

The dancing limbs of the young offender were uninjured in the jerk-and-swirl movement through the door. The door was trying to automatically close with the old-fashioned brass door closer that only worked slowly halfway. The end of the door closing action usually ended with a door slap to the rear of the entering party.

The outer office was holding a couple worn upholstered chairs. The school secretary's desk, which doubled as a barricade to the actual principal's office, was lost from sight due to a throng of mothers and children standing in wait for a turn with the secretary. It was no line. It was a mass that was forced to divide. Individuals were turning to either side depending on the art teacher's own steps.

He forced himself through in a serpentine trail like a snowplow in action, but out of control. Aartemann was leaving the wake of moms and tots to fill in behind, flowing like water behind a speedboat. If anyone spoke, he did not hear. Complete attention was on his quest of the inner office door.

It too, was made of heavy oak darkened from age with a top window. Clear enough glass to see a full room of seated adults. The door is shut—an "I'll dare you to penetrate" position as it is the principal's private office. The principal's desk is inside to the left in a corner not visible from the door window. Seated participants of the meeting are all with backs to the door. All but one lady. She, like the rest, is fixed of attention into the invisible corner.

Discouraged with the now obvious delay in discipline, Aartemann's mind whirls to plan B. Even in his outraged state, he had not nearly enough gumption to interrupt the sanctity of that closed-door meeting. *To plan B!* He placed (dropped) the guilty child on an oak plank bottom teacher desk chair abandoned in a small nook not ten feet from the principal's door. The hall tree, overgrown with winter attire temporally discarded by office staff, toppled and wobbled just a bit. It was grazed in his body spin. He would seek out the next best judge and executioner.

Her office is right next-door, and they have become friends as well as sympathetic colleagues. She could take the child. She could be made to hear and see the evidence—it was still clutched tightly in the right hand but now slightly crushed from the tenseness of the events. She will perform obligatory severe punishment.

The caustic trait of his Cobra-like mental venom and his race toward instant gratification (blood) in the form of justice left him with no thought as to what this punishment would be. *Perhaps a drawing and quartering as in Scottish Highland war history,* was ricocheting in his brain as an acceptable probability. *That seemed to work for the Scottish nuisance, Wallace. Expulsion was surely eminent. Pain to an extreme would be necessary to thwart any future recurrence of this type of infraction. Blood? Why not?*

Reason suddenly began to be a small portion of this scenario.

Oh, rats, the counselor would likely be in on such an important closed principal door conference, he concluded. The thought was surprising coming from a brain currently light of reasoning and sanity.

His eyes searched the door glass again seeing only what and who was visible earlier. *No doubt she would be in there. She would also be unavailable for this high-level discipline chore. There never seems to be a high command available when first graders are breathing arson.*

Moving further from his "fight or flight" brain stem reaction he began to further reason that she ... the sentence thought froze in place like a freight train running out of track in front of a mountain wall. It was instantly replaced with the memory that she was at the elementary school he serviced with art classes in another location, in another time, altogether dislocated from this place.

She is not the counselor here," he mentally mused. "She's not in the meeting. She'll never come out. She doesn't even exist at this place and cannot help me at this time. No, no, no! Abs, that is the school counselor at this elementary who must be found. Her office has an oak door, with dark aged varnish, and a carving in an insert panel below a frosted glass window that looked like a head, perhaps a child, and the crossed rulers glued directly below it creating a delightful sinister first impression entering the small dark room. A perfect place to take the arsonist.

His mind raced on but now with some thought, with some calculation involved, in planning, in question. *Is she in there? Should he go get the counselor out of the meeting? What should he tell her or should he just wait on the principal to finish the meeting? What is the rest of the class doing back downstairs in the art room?*

How long have I been gone from the art room? his thoughts finally return to earth, to responsibility and issues like negligence and professionalism.

In his mind he quickly decided he would just have to explain that "Tex" here was attempting to set fire to the project drawing paper by blowing on it. He would give the principal the evidence in his hand. Then he could return to class leaving punishment duty to the office staff. His conscious thought began talking back. That give and take of conversation for Mr. Aartemann was nothing new, and sometimes took on an audible quality leaving passers by at a loss.

His conscious thought, this time silently, said, *You can't tell the principal you left your room carrying a child to the office for severe punishment because he was setting fire to his paper by using his breath.*

But I will not tolerate that behavior in my classroom, some brain cell responded.

What? conscious cells again surfaced for the debate. *How? How do you breathe on paper and cause smoke and fire?*

He batted his eyes while considering that question for a moment or two. Common sense was telling him he needed to reevaluate what and how he needed to plead his case. He still felt the anger of the moment but his thinking was slowing to a more conscious pace. Aching eyes once again picked up the dusty green color of the walls from the early morning daylight's weak shine. He was more and more determined to win over this boy who so tested his authority.

He must be punished! Fainter mental anguish clung in his brain.

The five rows of filled bookshelves between window and door began also to focus to his right. The feelings of rage and anger were now diminishing to something more describable as disgust.

How could He?! What should I say? How? What? Wait, that's absurd, students don't breathe fire. What was ... and at almost that very point the reality of the bedroom bookshelves, the bedroom green, and the bedroom encounter become consciously clear. Mental stability is restored, at least to his normal level.

There is no smoking paper. The principal's office is only in his head. He has been wasting the first night of Christmas vacation with a dream of dragon-breath first graders. A dream of smoking art projects. Nightmares of inaccessible education administrators and the whole story is now recognized as unreal. He still is generating negative emotion as he lies awake in bed. His dream was wilder and more fanciful than *Peter Pan and Wendy* or *Alice in Wonderland.*

From *The Gentlewoman's Choice,* the Michael R. Phillips edited book of author George MacDonald published in 1882 originally as *Weighed and Wanting,* comes: "Yes, it was a dream, but do you think a dream is nothing at all? I think if it is a good dream, it must be God's. For you know every good thing is from God. He made the things that dreams and the things that set in dreaming, so He must be the master of dreams—at least when He pleases—and surely always of those who obey Him."

"So who mastered my dream?" the art teacher muses as he turns his heels to the side of the bed to arise into Christmas break. It is Christmas vacation and day one. There will be no students. Only a memory of the terrible fire-breathing first grade art student lingers. And soon that child's existence will cause much shared laughter as he tells his wife of his classroom to vacation transitional dream.

Now awake and alert he actually considers party mix for breakfast.

Delays and Cancellations

The day is beginning to feel like a day off from school. It takes three days of Christmas vacation to get acclimated to the holiday time off without students and duties. The day seems almost like summer break once again. Aartemann thinks how delightful it would be to be able to call in permanently sick after the holiday and remain on perpetual vacation even if the snow is falling.

I don't even mind the snow, he thinks to himself while sitting during an early morning in front of the studio computer. Checking email and surfing through eBay listings looking for nothing particular is pleasure. It's the best kind of buying. He finds many new authors for his library shelves that way. Aartemann, over the past year, found century-old books—cheap books but readable—by putting in search words like Irish, Scottish, croft, or kirk. The stronger the dialect in the stories, the better he likes the books. He now has fifty-four books on the "ready to read for the first time" shelf. All emit wondrous book mustiness and occasional leather smells that only very old books can.

Even at home the aging art teacher wanders off into a dream-like world. He mutters to himself. He imagines himself on the coasts of Ireland. Mild breezes blow across the winter waters and he skips stones toward jagged rocks surrounded with foam. He mentally converts Indiana snow drifts to ocean rolls. Half buried dead flowers killed by a Hoosier fall take on characteristics of Celtic seaweed awash with shells. His mind suddenly takes him to Scottish highlands as he walks with his imaginary plaid-wrapped, wild, red-haired companion. It takes little effort for him to skip to Biblical locations void of Midwestern harshness as he debates his own doctrines with the Zelots of that place and time.

Out the window he observes the family of four cats playing in the snow. The romping is at the rear of his property. The mother is Boots, named for the white chin bib and four white bootie looking feet on the otherwise black cat. Boots sits at the windless side of a weed caused drift. Aartemann's North Atlantic vision vanishes. Three offspring, who were often fed in the past summer, are playing in the titanium white fluff. They stand out against the white snow since one is all black and the other two dark tiger kittens. All three have their mother's markings in the white of the boots and bib. But the boots are buried in the two-inch snow today.

A little time passes thinking of the delights of summer, the time of freedom from employment, the time of reading, writing, artistic creations, and naps. He very quickly begins searching the web for sights offering information related to financial questions. Answers are yet needed about the possibility of retirement at the end of the school year term. The relaxation of Christmas break inspires him once again to work toward data. He looks for anything assuring him it will be okay to retire early. By the time the snow quits falling and the sun rises, he will have a generous stack of information to share with his slumbering wife. Retirement excitement is back in his head like an early Christmas gift from Old Nick.

The post New Year's first school week begins with a two-hour delay announced the night before. Evening called delays are a rare occurrence and happen only when the weather is beyond severe. A prior night's delay call is often followed with an extension or cancellation. Cancellation is not unexpected by morning. Snow is falling. Snow is blowing. It is bitter.

It is an easy call as the entire weekend was filled with a terrible mix of snow, freezing rain, cold, sleet, winds, and every imaginable nasty part of winter in Indiana. By Monday morning, today, school is cancelled early. The worst weather is yet approaching. It takes not a weatherman to see the increase in extreme conditions and depth of the white ground layer. It is a good day to get to stay home.

Tuesday is a repeat of Monday. Even the shoveling of Monday is repeated due to the blowing. Opened paths only drift over. The driveway clearing will wait for the snow, sleet, and wind to stop.

Every day of this week is started with a two-hour delay announced in the evening prior. It becomes routine with cancellation expected. The first three days are totally cancelled and now will have to be made up in the month of June. Unfortunately made up after the date when the schedule has called for summer break. The beginning of summer vacation! Thursday and Friday will be reduced by the two hours only. A late beginning saves the days from being rescheduled. But it is now only Wednesday. He holds his coffee cup steaming with fresh, hot, nutty-scented Starbucks and considers the outdoors from the warm inside of the house.

"I should go out and use the golf clubs and drive a few icicles over the drifts since I won't be able to play in June, due to the make-up days," the art teacher tells his wife while looking out the cold glass of the door to his patio.

Or more likely he is just talking to himself. She goes about a household task. He tries to help her a bit, but gets in the way. Housework not being his routine or expertise causes him to be of little help.

"I've come to not mind the 'snow days'—they are called that in the education world even if it is cold, or fog, or ice that causes the cancellation. I really mind little even though they are rescheduled on a warmer day," he tells his wife, Gail, thinking she is in the room.

Actually she has gone into the laundry room.

Oblivious of her departure he continues, "I don't fancy getting out in the bad weather and tempting the roads or the other drivers with no sense. The recovery time at home is even welcomed after falling on my pockets shoveling the garage apron. One should know better than to try shoveling six inches of snow with one hand and holding the newspaper with the other."

The image of him trying to read and shovel simultaneously is inaccurate. He was not reading. Warm smooth hard leather soles on wet ice under the new light snow were the real cause.

"The older I get as a teacher," he rambles on without looking for her presence, "the more I seem to act like the students of my elementary classes. Well, at least when I react to school closings, delays, vacations and holidays. I know in my brain that we will do 186 days of school in one form or another; at one time or another. It seems such a treat to get a five day weekend when it is not planned."

Should she be in hearing distance, she would agree, since the past days were a delight. They cook together, read together, watch movies from their private collection of DVDs and VHS tapes. Selection is not large but greater than a normal home due to more eBay transactions. There are lots of classics, Hallmarks, and romance chick-flicks that she likes. He's too proud to admit to enjoying them as a man. It is silly the way men fail to mature prior to the age of 117. Boys grow to men and remain human hero action figure mimes. Or like Pan, they never grow up.

"That may be the secret!"

Now Aartemann is not teacher or husband but a man definitely talking to himself. It can be concluded a sorry sight if someone was seeing him and hearing him. He squints at the white blowing out the windows.

"The unscheduled aspect of the time does not allow for filling the space with appointments. So the day, or in this case, days, becomes like Huck Finn racing off to the river raft. Ah, the life of a truant!"

And he laughs at the thoughts of himself, barefoot in the mud beside the river with a willow branch pole and cork bobber. Aartemann frequently imagines himself a Tom or Huck.

"Should I take down the Christmas tree?" he yells in the direction of his wife.

Finally he realizes she is no longer behind him in the same room.

"Do we have to?" she asks in a begging, whimpering replacement of a "No" answer.

He is relieved, but did not mention that.

Another situation, more related to an emotional experience than the wintry and physical attack upon his person, left him with one more reason for relishing a day snowed in at home. The emotional recovery is due to the time given him for reflection. That personal reflection time is thanks to God's Indiana winter weather presentation over the past few days. Stormy winter mix continues this day of Wednesday.

He relocates himself after refilling his cup of coffee. He couch sits, facing southward, and watches the snow flakes fly in several directions across the pond. Flake-fury is visible through the windows. The bare black wood's trees have limbs covered in white, like icing on a pretzel stick. Or better yet the pretzel sticks half dipped in white chocolate.

An occasional scarlet cardinal interrupts the colorless dreary cold woodscape but in general the scene has about as much life as the dead weeds now bent broken and covered in drifts. The desolation, loneliness, and despair of the winter blast on the outside of that living room wall reflect the near depression felt inside—within him. It is a curious thing to look upon. Feelings of helplessness swirling inside his mind match the flow of the flakes in the mix of winter winds. It happens to him, like today, out of the blue. It sometimes takes little to trigger a moment of depression. This attack is from a single phone conversation. It may last the day, or it may be gone in a flash. It can always return as quickly as it started and as suddenly as it departs. His depression sorties are like gatherer ants at a picnic, coming and going, and annoying.

Being physically comfortable due to legs wrapped in an antique quilt, an off-white, ivory color from age, it is easy to reflect on the loneliness and isolation that might have been felt by early Hoosier pioneers of the area. They likely looked out their own door of a log cabin in the midst of a similar mid-winter storm. With no life apparent in front of them; they would have seen exactly the view across this world's, this day's, this place's pond. Only they would have the knowledge that the woods and the trees would go on for miles and miles before another human could be found or another house or hut would provide protection. They had no chance to escape the isolation.

For this snowed-in art teacher, the existence of a town with all the modern superstores and conveniences lay just outside the wall on the far side of the living room. He is opposite that pioneer in that his isolation is but a convenience of a warm stay-at-home availed through the duration of unpleasant snowy winds.

His discouragement is simply from a conversation. It is a misunderstanding over the phone from the night before. It will pass as the winds give way to the beauty of soft drifts of snow. That will prompt a different form of softness within. Additional weather will extend the self-imposed isolation that will turn into restful opportunity. One step precedes the next till the depression feelings abate.

His fresh time, still home bound by weather, is eventually transformed into a reading and writing experience that delights and enlightens. Pages are turned in books and in journals that reward the time spent with them. It's perhaps an easy thing for him, a teacher; but would it have been so for the pioneer? He pauses to reflect but unable to answer.

He journals words on empty lined pages of a cloth covered journal. Its outer hard book cover is patterned with violet shimmering dragonflies. The journal had been purchased from the reduced table at Barnes and Noble while busy with Christmas shopping for others. He likes buying himself small gifts, has great difficulty selecting gifts for others, and gets embarrassed at receiving a gift. He is unlikely to ever try to figure out why. He is never that shy in front of his class.

Between the dragonfly covers of the book he reflects on words penciled about his students.

> How is their day compared with my own? Will they find contentment in the time off? How many will opt for TV over a book? Will any of them look past the fierceness of the storm and find a peaceful delight? Will their mind's imagination be limited to a controller made to transmit signals from fingers to game screen, or a video player, or some other box requiring no brain input? Will they be alone? Will any use art materials at home? How many have none? Will they be alone? Will parents be gone? Will they be alone today? If not, will they feel alone? Will parental employment isolate them inside a modern cabin with little more to stimulate than the activities of boredom? Would some of my students prefer the school to home? Abuse?

It is a while till his eyes return to the journal having spent much time staring at swimming snowflakes in upper windows. He sees them but does not think of them. His mind is on the students and the unknown answers.

He writes on,

> I have conquered a bit of life that was once for me a frustration. I manage, thanks to modern invention, better than a pioneer. I achieve in a time when my student may waste. I have attained ability covetable by some. A winter advisory predicts weekend inches additionally. I will sport a smile if a phone call comes on Sunday night: "There is a two-hour delay for Monday."

> A previous night's call of a two-hour delay gives opportunity for a late night read or a movie into the nighttime that normally would have been used for sleep. The alarm can be off since daylight will do the awakening chore in a much more gracious way than the suddenly noisy radio, even one tuned to a Christian station. That inward alarm, the habit of rising to a regular hour, minute, can often get me awake even quicker than the radio set a full half hour earlier than needed. Or another delay day awakening jolt can be the early unexpected phone call announcing via the school staff phone-tree that the delay is now a cancellation, a delight to hear at first, until the reality of a make-up requirement for the lost day will now take place on what was to be a June summer day. Summer vacation! Sun time!

> And so the winter school days have passed with interruptions. Two consecutive weeks, ending one month and bringing in another, each ended with

three cancellations following delays, a two-hour delay that remained just two, and only one full normal school day. That causes, now, six additional full days of school beyond Memorial Day, called Decoration Day by my parents—a full week into June's summertime that had been planned.

I am able to adjust quickly and enjoy the days off even though I have to sit inside and look out windows rather than spend them like I would in June, reading on the patio with an occasional golf outing. Yes, the days are fine for this aging teacher that now better appreciates the ability to remain at home in bad winter conditions as compared to sledding over the river and through the woods to elementary school. This past two week snow and ice spell landed me on my pockets once while shoveling one handed, and once on my hands and side while hurrying to the truck over ice covered gravel. It was good none observed my very ungraceful slips. It was even better that no severe injuries occurred—just soreness and a couple of hand scratches.

After these two winter weeks plus the additional weekend, his radio alarm is finally needed to arouse for a full day of school. He is awakened after a good night's sleep, following a loving peaceful drifting off where he slumbered into unconsciousness while silently praying. He was blessed with a gentle back rub from his love as he prayed. He rejoiced experiencing the presence of his God within. The radio wakes him with his arms about her. God is still feeling as close as she. Prayer, mostly of thanksgiving, is on his motionless lips. A desire develops for another cancellation. If only the moment did not have to end the hour just passed (an hour being the absolute limit) till the embrace was broken in favor of shaving, brushing, showering, dressing, eating and coffee. That is the habitual procedure of the day's beginning in preparation for this arriving day of teaching employment.

It would take two hours to try to explain the love/peace emotion within that embrace. It is so beyond a morning husband and wife hug. The Holy Spirit is once again wrapped around it and tapestried through it. He does teaching fairly well, but they do married awesomely.

"God's at the core," he states when he is asked why.

"Greetings!"

"Greetings!" he repeats over and over as students file from busses.

All enter stomping their snowy boots on mats, and see their art teacher, Mr. Aartemann, standing inside with coveralls, large pink mittens, lime green earmuffs, and a hat designed a decade or two earlier than the birth of those students' parents.

"Hello, Mr. Aartemann. Are you cold?"

"Brr-rr! Welcome to the North Pole," he returns.

"Greetings!"

"Greetings!"

"Greetings!" he continues to repeat, as students come

in, stomp, stare, and just move on likely thinking, *We're back to school, and so is Mr. Aartemann. He's weird.*

"Greetings!"

He grabs a fallen child.

"Are you okay? Slowly does it, the floor is wet from all the snow. Did you make a snowman?"

"Greetings!"

Later in the day Gail Aartemann, his wife, tries with words sent e-mail to his desk computer, to express her joy over much time spent together during snowy blustery winter days. He decides that perhaps she said what he would have, or should have said.

> I've been praying for you throughout this morning, asking the Lord to cause you to feel His love for you, and also mine. What an awesome God we have, and what an awesome love He has given us to share, three-way. I've been pretty speechless before Him this morning, as I tried to pray. Words fail. Worship alone provides the means of relaying my thoughts and feelings. It all started last night ... did I tell you I love you? I do!
>
> —G

Only God knows at this time that school closings due to weather are finished for this school year. It will be months before humans realize the fact. Due to human ignorance, none cheer.

Ruler Abuse

The students walk into the art classroom with Mr. Aartemann sitting behind the computer doing what Mr. Aartemann does all the time behind the computer screen.
Mr. Aartemann has procedures. There is a correct procedure for entering the studio quietly, arriving at individual
assigned seats without a peep and remaining so until he
emerges from his hiding spot. Only then will instruction
begin for this period's work. This particular second grade
class' entry is perfect. Some of the classes pride themselves
on doing that. Some even attempt to sneak into the room
without him seeing them, or hearing their entry. It never
works because he has strategically located sight paths on
both sides of the monitor and through the stacks of books,
videos, and other items on the shelves acting as a parti-
tion directly in front of his computer desk. But to please
the class and reinforce the correct entry behavior, he often
pretends to a colossal surprise. They like that!

No one really knows if Mr. Aartemann became an art
teacher because of his name or if he had his name changed
in a courtroom. Or if he made it up just for teaching days
and on other days when school is not in session he is just
Mr. Smith or Mr. Jones or Mr. Wilson. Maybe his name
is something terrible like Mr. Archabolandrietti that no
human being could ever learn to spell or even speak correctly. Maybe he is an escaped prisoner who learned to
draw pictures in a jail cell. Maybe he is hiding from the
police. Maybe he is an alien from the Twelfth Star of Gan.

He was beamed down to earth and is on a secret mission to gather pictures of life on the planet Earth and someday will just disappear and be sporged back to 12*G, as his real home is known outside the Milky Way. No one really knows.

Timmy Small once questioned his humanness due to the size of his nose.

"Excellent entry, class," he utters as he salutes the class while rising from his teacher chair on wheels. "I need you to come into all the other classes and demonstrate the proper procedure for art arrival. Well done!"

Smiles visualize the pride in the class of students. They sit up a bit straighter and peer intently at him each desiring to outdo the entry with perfect "active listening" skills. They are ready to work and eager to please.

"Remember what we talked about in the last class? Do you remember the two artists' paintings that we talked about last week? What kind of drawing did the artists do that we are going to try?"

"Towns!" a student shouts without waiting on their hand to get raised or waiting to be called on for an answer. The rest of the students with hands in the air slowly lower them dejected for a lost opportunity.

"But what was used to make the towns?" Mr. Aartemann further questions. "Thank you for raising your hand," and he points to Mandi without calling her name because he always has difficulty remembering all of the several hundred student names he has each year.

"Paint."

"I mean ... well, correct. But I mean, how did they make the street seem to look like it got farther and farther away? It is called one point ..." he hesitates and watches for hands to go up.

Delay in calling upon a student's answer continues after the first couple of hands are raised, thus giving others time to think for themselves.

" ... Okay, everybody together, one point ..."

"*Perspective*," about a dozen students shout out, along with a few simultaneous insertions of "perspection" and "prescription" and "perteckrive."

"Good. One point perspective—you need to remember that. And you will by the time we get our towns drawn using—*one point perspective*."

Mr. Aartemann really emphasizes the words.

"Hold up your hand with fingers telling me how many times you have helped. It looks like we still have some twos that need a turn, so everyone with three and four fingers up need to put their hands down. Five! How did you get to help five times already? Do I like you best? Here, we'll split the projects, you hand out these and Cami, you find owners for this pile." (Groans from those not chosen.) "Bobby, you got muscles today? Show me! Good! Give everyone one of these rulers ... fast ... don't let them pick the color, you just give them one."

Thus with the tools and projects being handed out, Mr. Aartemann turns and heads to the music stand he uses as a teaching lectern.

"Tartar sauce!" is the comment.

Those unusual "cursing" oaths uttered in disgust and disappointment for not getting to help come from a good student. It is not said in anger but just from impatience for his opportunity to help. It sometimes seems quite possible that an elementary student could die from dejection at the age of eleven or twelve if they never get a single chance to help the art teacher distribute something to their class.

Mr. Aartemann turns to the child, raises his shoulders in a shrug with fists clenched, drops the shoulders as the fists plunge down as well and simply retorts, "Grape juice!"

It only reinforces in the children his weirdness.

"Now, what is a ruler used for?" he asks.

Hands go up all over the room, one child's hand is chosen by Aartemann and the reply is "Measuring."

"And?"

He points; she answers, "Straight lines."

"Perfect!" he concludes. "Now you probably won't believe this but there have been some students, second grade students just like yourself that have used the ruler for other purposes. We only use the rulers for measuring and for making straight lines. Is anyone going to use it like a tomahawk?"

No hands are raised, but giggles sound.

"Somebody actually tried to do that and I had to take the ruler away. They had to make a town with no straight edge. They had all crooked lines and the town looked like it had been hit by a tornado. Is anyone going to turn the ruler into a drumstick and beat on the pencil can or on the table edge? Good, because a second grader did that once and it put nicks on the side of the ruler and then the ruler would not make straight lines. Is anyone going to sword fight?"

Mr. Aartemann demonstrated a sword thrust and strike motion.

"It's a good thing because when the swords, I mean rulers, hit together both of them end up with nicks and then … no more straight lines. Is anyone going to play baseball? Is anyone going to try to golf?"

Each sport is demonstrated with a swing appropriate to the game.

"Is anyone going to do this?" and at this point he places the ruler's center hole over the point of a pencil and pretends to start the ruler spinning.

"A helicopter, are you going to turn it into a helicopter?"

"No-o-o," the class answers in unison.

It is a good sign they are still with him.

"Do you know why that is so dangerous?"

Again a chorus of drawn out no-o-o's interrupts his pause.

"Look at this ruler. See how it is shaped? It is just like the wing of a big airplane. It's flat on the bottom and slightly rounded on top. When the airplane moves down the runway, picking up speed with engines, the air currents flow under the wing and over the wing and curl around a bit behind."

Mr. A. demonstrates while talking.

"The jet then gets going fast enough that the plane lifts off because of the air currents. They call the air it floats on 'lift.' That is how the plane filled with all those big people and all of their luggage can fly through the air. Now since this ruler is shaped the same as the wings, if you get the ruler spinning on top of the pencil fast enough the air currents will flow under the wing, oops I mean ruler, and over the wing, oops I mean ruler and the currents will swirl a bit behind the wi-i-i … oops I mean ruler. And if you spin it fast enough the ruler will get lift and it will lift off the pencil and it will fly."

The class is intent and looking excited as if it should be time right now for the demonstration of the flying ruler.

"Don't do it! It may fly right into your eye. Or hit someone else! Or at the very least hit the can or the edge of the table and leave a notch in the edge of the wing, oops the ruler, and then it cannot help you make a straight line for your one point perspective town. You see …" (Here is a long pause for emphasis and a wait till silence is again complete.) " … *the ruler's got no pilot!*"

The students erupt into laughter. But they get the point and without a doubt there will be no flying of helicopters happening in the art room for another year. The helicopter pilots have been grounded.

"Now we need to make straight lines," he states pulling the students back to the project underway but as yet hardly with a significant start. "You already had made the one line up and down between the top and bottom dots we measured in the last class time. You also should have two long lines reaching from the center dot on one side of the paper across to the opposite top and bottom corners of the paper. The result looks a bit like a capitol 'A' that tripped and fell on its side, right? It probably ate too much lunch and got too fat to stand up right ... Maybe not!"

The students listen intently and watch eagerly as he demonstrates on the board the use of vertical lines drawn with the ruler to make sides of buildings for the street scene. He explains carefully to them the need to align the ruler with the left and right edges of the paper. And to make sure the sides of all drawn buildings, windows, doors, signs and other things are exactly straight up and down on the paper.

"Vertical!" he introduces the word, not really expecting second grade students to all remember the word or the meaning. But a couple will.

"If you make the sides of your buildings slanted, not exactly up and down, it will look like a hurricane passed by. Do you know what a hurricane is?"

A few nods happen.

"If you make your door sides slanted, it will look like the fat lady from the circus tried to get through and pushed" (Aartemann pronounced 'pooshed' from Hoosier habit) "it over. If you make the sides of the windows leaning and not straight up and down, vertical, it will appear that a truck ran into the building and knocked the window out."

Each of his statements gets a giggle from many of the class' students, then he continues, "I got hit by a truck once and that's why I lean" (he demonstrates), "or maybe it's because I'm old ..." (that gets two laughs), " ... well, maybe not."

"The tops and bottoms of the buildings point to the dot. Tops and bottoms point to the first dot you measured on the side of the paper. Do you find it? Yes, that's right! Now the top and bottom of all the buildings will be the two lines already drawn. Yes, those two long lines that went from the dot to well ... it's called a vanishing point ... the dot is ... because the buildings appear to vanish or disappear there ... anyhow. Building tops and bottoms are from the dot to the top and bottom corners of the paper on the opposite side. Confused? Got it? Yes, that's right! Now, when you put a top on a door, or the top and bottom of a window is drawn, those lines also go where?"

Hands go up by nearly half the class and a couple speak right up without being called on, "To the dot!"

"Gregory, thanks for raising your hand, how do you draw the top and bottom lines of doors and windows?"

"To the dot!"

"Exactly, thanks. Now the top and bottom of signs also go to the dot. As a matter of fact, anything with straight lines that are really flat lines on your buildings will point to the dot. The dot is the vanishing point. Sides of things go straight up and down, tops and bottoms to the dot."

He points to a student and asks, "How do you do the sides?"

"Up and down."

He points to another. "How do you draw the tops and bottoms?"

"To the dot."

He points, "Sides?"

"Up and down."

"Good," points to another, "Bottoms and tops?"

"To the dot."

"Good, use the ruler and go to work. Remember this

is work, hard work, do not have fun, do not pass go, do not collect two hundred … oh well … it is time for hard work. Go to work!"

Students quickly grab the rulers placed prior to their arrival beside the gallon industrial size tin cans in the middle of the table. Mr. Aartemann has converted cans to supply storage containers by painting a color on the outside. This also allows for a table of students to be identified as a group just by naming a color. They are eager to begin their first building for their town and ideas are already racing through their youthful brains. Cells dream all of the different kinds of stores, offices, shops, and businesses they will place on their street drawing. Most probably have more ideas spinning inside them than the paper size will allow. It will likely only hold about three buildings, four at the most. That is what he already informed them. In their excitement, they did not hear. But each will soon find out the limit.

One student begins with a candy store and the door is leaning. Mr. Aartemann points it out and the erasing begins. Another student begins with a dentist's office, a bit of a surprise when he looks directly at the student and realizes her smile shows more gaps than it does teeth. Perhaps several trips to the dentist have been recent. Perhaps that accounts for the idea. Another is making their own family's gift shop located in a local town. More than one begins with a theater, which was one of the buildings demonstrated by him, Aartemann. He does not like the copying but will only suggest that the rest of the buildings should be something they think of out of their own brain.

"Do not steal from the example on the chalkboard," he'd like to scream.

He just says it. Calmly. And they listen. And they will obey.

Mr. Aartemann walks about the room looking over shoulders at the progress of so many town pictures. A few problems occur here and there. For the most part, the one-point perspective seems to be going quite well for second grade students. He suggests doubling lines on a window here and there. A student forgot to double lines around the door to detail the casing. He spells a word here and there for students. He sympathizes with spelling needs since he's not a bee champ himself. He was in a school spelling bee once and went out on his first word: cloud.

"C-L-O-W-D."

He will never forget it. He was embarrassed. All the practice on huge words was wasted. Spellcheck was initially invented for Aartemann. Maybe by the vice-president!

"B-Λ-K-E-R-Y."

"Pizza has two z's, John."

"The s on your bike shop sign is backward."

"O-o-o-o, nice job! Are you a professional artist?"

"Oh boy, a bookstore. I love to go into bookstores. Can I go to yours? Yes, how about a discount on all the books that I buy?" he teases while appreciating another excellent effort on a shop drawing.

He really would covet a discount at a bookstore. He enjoys a book as much as a painting.

"Finish getting that erased and then I'll show you something," he encourages while laying a hand on the shoulder of Beth. Tiny little Beth is really an Elizebeth.

Elizebeth with three e's instead of two e's and an a! Elize-beth MacNeil is a struggler for mediocrity and will proba-bly never attain high honors. Yet she's a quiet worker who silently sits doing her best. At least what she thinks is best. She fails to ask for help when it is needed. Perhaps she fails to recognize the need. She is the picture of a second grade Irish student with her less than perfectly combed orange-red hair and freckled nose that invades the higher part of her cheeks as well. The freckles almost match the hair color. She would have made a perfect extra for the filming of the movie *Tis* based on the prize-winning book of the same name. All she needs is clothing slightly more bedraggled and a good bit dirtier. She is a clean girl, just a bit disheveled. She could be the school's St. Patrick's Day poster child. Aartemann would like the school to actu-ally have such a thing. He'd enjoy it if the school actually did anything related to St. Patrick's Day other than hav-ing a potato bar in the teacher's lounge and lunchroom with everyone pitching in with "Hoosier Pot-Luck" style of toppings. That normally satisfies the art teacher. He's a lover of gooed-up taters. He's constantly claiming more Irish lineage than genealogically allowed. There is more pride in Irish chromosomes. Or, maybe it is the soda bread he often enjoys that is going to his brain.

"Now, Beth, try it like this. Here, see how I've lined up this point with the dot at the edge of the page?" he points. "Hold the ruler yourself now, I'm going to let go. No, not there, look, if you hold it there and try to run the pencil along the edge it will move when you get toward the other end and the line will be crooked. Hold it in the center. Hold it between the ends of the line you want to draw. Hold it down against the paper tight and then make the line."

Beth takes over on the ruler once again. She begins the line just as the ruler slips slightly away from the direction of the vanishing point. Aartemann ignores the slight shift, it being not enough for him to stop her progress. Then about half way toward the completed line her pencil leaves the edge of the ruler. She still holds tightly to the paper with a white-knuckle pressure, and the pencil line meanders farther and farther away from the ruler's guiding ability. The child's mark makes a definite hook and within three inches is headed in a perpendicular direction from the ruler.

He exasperates, "Stop!"

Good, I didn't shout, he thinks.

Silly, Illy, Elizebeth. You are supposed to keep the pencil against the ruler to make a straight line. That's why we are using the ruler. For straight lines! You cannot use a ruler for those S and J and curvy lines. You cannot make a loop-d-loop line head to the vanishing point. It has to be a straight line. Use the ruler. Use the pencil by touching the ruler as you draw the line. Silly, silly, silly! Let me look at those roots on that red hair. Ah, there I see the problem, blonde roots. Now I understand why you put the ruler on this side of the paper and draw the line on the other side. Blonde roots ... Mr. Aartemann thinks much later, after the class. Honestly he was not truthfully thinking it at all but just sees the humor in the confusion for the child. He would never really say anything even close to a statement like that to a student.

What he really said when Beth's pencil left the straight side of the ruler was, "You did really fine on the first part of that line. Now let's work together and see if we can get the whole line perfect. I think we can. I think you can. I *know* you can do it. Here, let me help. Hold the ruler with me ... good, now start the pencil moving along the ruler, s-l -o-w-l -y, good, slowly, great, keep going, wonderful, almost done so keep watching the side of the ruler, good job, ah, that's it! You did it! Now, try the next one by yourself, I'll just watch. Doing well. Keep going! *Yes! Yes!* You can do it. Excellent job. Now you're on your own. Just take it slow and watch what you're doing because you can make them straight ... if you use the ruler."

He pats her on the shoulder as he leaves to check out the tables on the other side of the room. He does not miss the gigantic Irish smile that flows across her face. Somewhere above St. Patrick also smiles down.

"What happened to that window?" he jokes with a boy on the far table near the corner.

The picture is well underway and all seems in good perspective with the exception of a large window on the second floor. An unusual window is on the "TaTwo Parler" the student is including in his own fictitious town.

Why on earth does he want a Tattoo Parlor in his town? the teacher thinks.

"Tattoo Parlor is spelled t-a-t-t-o-o p-a-r-l-Oh-r" instead he spells aloud. "Do you like tattoos?" he asks the lad.

"Yah, my step-dad got one on his arm while he was in the navy. It's cool! I want to get a dinosaur on my arm when I'm old 'nuff," he answers and brightens in the face with the reply.

"Ah, that explains it," Mr. Aartemann quietly murmurs

as he moves on trying not to make verbal, moral or preference judgments.

"Awesome, Samantha" but since there is no sign of recognition of his comment he repeats, "Awesome, Samantha" and touches her paper in front of her.

He can not for the life of him understand why her parents and family call her Sam when her name is Samantha. She is a pretty girl and deserves to be called Samantha, not Sam. But the students know her by Sam, and call her that. She usually writes Sam on her school work. Lately it has been noticed by him that art work is being handed in with Samantha Williams 2R in the corner. Mr. Aartemann always calls her Samantha. She seems to like it enough that she is using it herself—on her art.

Mr. Aartemann is a bit old fashioned. The cause is his age. He truly believes that Sam, and Bobby, and Ricky are boy's names although he has female students that have been given or go by those first names. He wonders why their parents could not have just used some of his favorite girl names like: Heather, Noel, Whisper, Cherokee, and Alette, all actual former students with names he is proud of. But he never openly discusses his opinion on this.

Sometimes he does mummer disapprovals while sitting behind the monitor and books and tapes and the hourglass timer with the pink sand.

She looks up, smiles and says, "Thanks."

"Oh my, we're late!" he exclaims with exaggerated alarm.

He knows there is yet three minutes till the next class will arrive. They may not even be on time.

"Put the rulers in the cans, put the pencils in the cans, put the erasers in the cans, well, you know how to do it.

Hand your projects to the end of the rows of tables toward the door, please. Do it as quickly as you can, we're late, it's my fault, so help me out and do it quickly and quietly. Blue table, good, line up. Red, you're next, thanks for being so quick and quiet. Brown. Yellow. Pink."

"We don't have a pink table," the remaining students respond.

"I know that! I was just checking you. Good problem solving. Good thinking. Smart class! Black," and with the final can color call, the remainder of the class lines up in parallel lines in front of the door.

"See you after Christmas" he calls after them as they exit.

Silently he wonders if they will mentally register that the holiday mentioned is weeks past. A hand gives them a wave. "Duh" expressions slowly being to emerge on the faces of several that heard and turned to look. He just shrugs and races to put away their towns and prepares for the eminent coming of the following group of eager art students.

As he puts away the rulers collected from the tables' supply cans, he remembers again, and re-wonders, and smiles that once again a student will hold down a ruler for a straight line but make the line in another place other than directly against the ruler's edge. It happens at least once in almost every class. For some students, perhaps a plastic helicopter is the best use of a twelve-inch ruler.

Art Valentine Party

The next class arrives but he has yet to rid himself and the art room of the kindergartners. Attempted is a single file line with projects in hand waiting at the door. One kinder is bent over trying to tie a shoe with very little success. He falls over. The last student in the kinder line, an overweight boy with a project already torn nearly in half, meanders in the direction of the kiln. He acts as though twenty-three seconds standing in line is quite enough for any human to endure. The classroom teacher, Francis Peiper, is two minutes late and the art schedule calls for a change of classes without the benefit of a normal five minute span between the two coming and going sessions. That is the normal situation. Schedules in art allow for the transfer and reset and re-supplying of the art room for another group. That is the normal plan. Normal in practice is what is now taking place. Back to back is a back breaker.

"Joel, get the picture out of your mouth. The colors are running down your chin now. Do you want to go home looking like a clown?" Aartemann asks a line that is now still single file but serpentine.

If Mrs. Peiper does not arrive quickly, the single file will be lost to something looking more like the first day of marching practice for a Civil War Army infantry corp.

"Billy West! Don't touch the kiln buttons! It might blast off and the pilot is not yet in his seat down inside of it. Back in line! Over here! Pronto!"

Billy meanders, but south not east, toward the line.

Normally the youngest class is by now strolling down the hall with a bit of a continuing slalom line due to gawkers positioned between followers. It is always a bit of a delight to get a secret look at a kinder class that is taking its time from one place to another. Aartemann believes a few could wander right into a classroom while passing an open door. And perhaps never be noticed as missing by the rest of the class. At least until classroom roll call.

"Where is Mrs. Peiper?" Aartemann rhetorically asks the kinders.

He directs them to a hallway line outside the art room door.

The next class, the group that has been waiting in two parallel lines against the hall wall begins to enter. A third grade teacher coming out of the teachers' lounge adjoining the art room approaches Aartemann. The hall wall supports his lean. He watches the new class enter his room.

"Our class was working on a lesson on simile yesterday."

Mr. Aartemann tries not to look puzzled, wondering what the request is about to be. Teachers approaching him usually mean some need for assistance in a poster or something similar. He hopes his failure to remember the meaning of the word simile does not show on his face.

"We went around the room giving examples of similes."

"Uh, huh?" he says.

Ignorance clutches his brain. He never was good at vocabulary. Or spelling. Good cover, he thinks.

"I thought this was excellent and you'd enjoy it also. Tim's example was: 'Mr. Aartemann decorates paper like a snowflake decorates the air.' Isn't that good?"

Brain cells scan picture files. He has no idea or mental picture as to which student Tim is. He does like the sentence.

"Mr. Aartemann decorates paper like a snowflake decorates the air." He repeats the words with a smile and follows it with a thank you. "I'll have to remember that one. Thanks. Better get this class working. Thanks again."

Later in the day it is a fifth grade class that has to wait for their art room opportunity. Mrs. Peiper repeats the late pick-up of her afternoon class just as she had done in the morning session. While standing in the hall outside the studio entry a discussion is concerning which direction the hyper Peiper afternoon kindergarten class will march. It makes a difference as to which side of the hall the fifth grade students will decide to make their future waiting line. Since this has become a habit of overlapping time a new procedure for waiting is decided upon. Ponderings and decisions are made. About the same time the kinder teacher, Pieper, has arrived and begins piping her class of pickled peppers down the hall.

Fifth grade is in a festive mood having come directly from preparing for their Valentine party. Those activities will take place immediately after art class. Sometimes, especially with younger classes, this preannounced festival activity creates a complete lack of on-task ability for students. Minds are more attuned to the upcoming treats and games than on shapes and colors for art.

Once the fifth graders have sole possession of his attention they challenge Mr. Aartemann with a riddle.

"What did the painter say to her boyfriend?" is the question presented even before the last student sets pockets to a seat.

It seems to come with an attitude that if the art teacher incorrectly gives the answer, then they all will reverse their direction, return to their regular room at the opposite far end of the hall and begin to party hardy.

Aartemann wants to guess the answer. He can never explain why that is suddenly important but he wants to surprise the class and get it right. At least, at the very least, he should have a response or alternate answer as clever as what they will produce. It will not jump to mind for him. And he is given precious little time to think. The class of eleven year olds wants to stump him as much as he wants to look smart.

Unlike the verbalizing of the riddle, which came from the classroom teacher as spokesperson, the class speaks the correct answer in unison. It is spoken as carefully as the presentation of lines in a stage play. The unison delivery almost carries with it a tune—something not unlike a Broadway musical portion. This obviously has been rehearsed. Aartemann's ignorance was expected.

"I love you with all my art."

All are delighted that Aartemann can not guess. By the time the class gets the seven words out as an answer the words crescendo to a near shout that surely can be heard in the classroom nearest the art room. That classroom is above.

All he can now do is groan. He imagines that will suffice for his ignorance and lack of quick wit. Actually catching the art teacher off guard without a reply proves more delightful yet for the majority of the pack. So he doesn't really mind playing the fool.

The riddle is now presented. It is hand written on a three-inch red construction paper heart sporting nine paper punched holes on the top heart humps. Eight are holding Dumdum suckers in a variety of flavors including chocolate, cotton candy, mystery (goofy name for a flavor), others, and one called bubble gum that he will not ever attempt to eat. If asked, Aartemann would likely allude that a sucker in the flavor of bubble gum is a sin not to be indulged in. One student later guesses his favorite flavor, crème soda, which is not among the offerings. Keith gives him his own personal Valentine addressed to the art teacher. Attached is a cherry Lifesaver lollipop. Mr. Aartemann eats it in class.

Nearly every student also presents him with a hug as they pass him in the room, leaving their seats for the intended occasion. There was a time when student hugs were fearful and shunned. They were considered a short step from an ugly rumor and eventual firing. In the wrong place and at the wrong time it still can be. But today's planned or likely impromptu reception line of hugs resembles more of a party type thing, like a wedding celebration, or at a graduation open house, rather than sick dirty old man antics. It is a feel good. It is warm fuzzies. Initiated by the students or perhaps encouraged by their leader, their teacher, it takes place while she is a witness of no ill intent.

This is the extent of any Valentine party in the art room. A pair of boys enter in the final period of the day with an option of white cupcake with white icing swirled on top like a Dairy Queen cone and sprinkled with pink, white, and red tiny heart sugar wafers—very small—or the choice of a chocolate with swirled chocolate frosting and identical sprinkles. He chooses the white. He eats it since it is certain the cakes are store bought and safely baked in a clean environment. It's a sad condition that teachers have to now consider the safety of a party offered cupcake.

During the fifth grade class Mr. Aartemann receives email as a result of his morning cell phone call.

> Hi, sweetie!!!! Wow, three gorgeous red roses just came for me, from you! Thank-you, they truly are gorgeous! So hard to believe it's another Valentine's Day together. How blessed I am to have you to share my life with. You are the air I breathe, my warmth, my nourishment, and my heart-home. I love you. See you soon. Thanks you again for the flowers.

He smiles, delighted to have surprised Gail.

"Great art room party this year" he says aloud at the end of the school day.

No one hears. Everyone is having his and her Valentine party at their own location. He celebrates alone thinking of the evening to be spent with Gail.

"I have got to decide on the retirement thing. I need to write a letter if I intend to do it. I need to decide. Oh Lord, help me decide." Aartemann's only decision is to put it off and head home to Gail and a home Valentine supper.

Thanks to a stainless steel travel cup decorated with I Chronicles 4:10, The Prayer of Jabez, his fingers have warmed enough to remove the winter gloves. It sounds like a February break from snow shoveling but instead he sits at his teacher's desk awaiting the arrival of students. The cupcake wrapper dropped from yesterday's afternoon party leftover, sits crumpled amid crumbs on his desk. He puts it in the waste container and licks off sticky frosting residue from his fingertips. Prognosis for the return of power to this school is "maybe" two hours. The power company bases that on one hour of labor after their arrival. Arrival is not intended for another hour yet. Aartemann's recollection about the punctuality of utility crews has them ranked in his mind right in there with general practitioners and an end of the day doctor's office appointment when a long hour wait is again extended beyond the next meal.

He finds a thermometer in a drawer of his teacher's desk and he is pleased to see that it is not swollen fat with hoarfrost. It reads forty-five degrees Fahrenheit until he fondles it with his hands that have been given their warming spurt by the stainless mug of Starbucks.

When he first entered the building he was unaware of a power problem. The hallowed halls did seem a bit darker but the coolness was yet undeterminable under his fauve down coat plus the fact that outside temperature was in single digits. A student, a child of one of the staff, rounded the corner where he stood. He made the proud announcement, excited to be the bearer of tidings.

"The power's off!"

It still has not registered since the entrance has one wall of glass and the opposite is also largely glass with a glass door leading to a courtyard. Here he stands in more light than exists anywhere else in the building. He turns toward the office area which is not his normal route through the structure. Awareness sets in and he now begins to notice the lack of artificial light. A room he passes is totally black beyond the first four feet into the windowless space. He enters the workroom to pick up his mail and discovers he can not even see the mailboxes on the wall, let alone the names to indicate which cubby to draw from. Through an attached office room and to the far side of the school office he can see the outline of the door that enters into the main lobby of the school. It is also lit well by daylight through ample outside windows. He escapes by that route, slowly.

In the lobby chairs huddle coated staff members. These earliest arrivers already are in conversation over the condition of a school without power as well as the loss of a former staff member's husband.

"It's been off at least since 6:00 A.M"

"How come the hall emergency flood lights are not on?"

"They were earlier but now we're getting some daylight in."

"They're trying to decide right now."

"What's to decide? It's freezing in here, no light, no water, no restrooms."

Already Aartemann regrets the half pot of coffee gulped down within the past hour. It is working into his system. This could be a case for the Emergency Bladder Control Unit.

"Today was to be the convocation!"

"No problem. It's an Abe Lincoln enactment. He's used to no heat."

"And no lights."

"How are we going to fix lunch?"

"I've got some peanut butter," offers the young lad who is the son of a staffer.

It is the same lad that revealed in announcing to Mr. Aartemann the no power news upon his earlier entrance.

"Let's go see how light it is in the classrooms. I can live with no heat for a couple of hours."

It is not exactly a welcome statement to most sitting in the hall since it comes from the principal in discussion with another administrative figure. They are obviously deciding upon the continuation of this school day.

"They need to get the announcement on the radio before parents leave."

"This would not have to be made up like the snow days."

"Glad I've got my coffee."

A half dozen are again walking the halls that make a complete circle around this floor of the building. Some of them do it regularly for exercise. Today it adds warmth and the walker flock grows with the laps.

"The fifth grade has been doing a Yukon Iditarod Trail theme but this seems such an extreme."

"If my house got this cold I'd go to a motel."

"We could leave in mass with chill spasms and violent coughing and ask 'them' to call a sub once the power comes on to activate the phone system again."

Nothing works, not even emergency desired technology like a telephone. Only cell phones connected the school with civilization beyond the tundra.

Of course there is ample joking with one forming lips in an oval for blowing breath rings in the hall's cool air. Outdoor restroom privileges are suggested in jest with ladies to the parking lot side of the building and the boys opposite where trees are most prevalent.

The cold for faculty and staff begins to become finger numbing. Most are wearing the coats and gloves they arrived in. Some wish they had worn more.

Students arrive a good bit puzzled why the teachers, staff and even the principal are greeting them in coats and gloves. When they file out of the lobby area, bright from day-lighted windows, and enter halls heading toward classrooms, their heads turned upward. Heads spin around wondering, obviously, about the darkness only now apparent.

The convocation, a dramatization by a regional man quite skilled at performing solo as Abe Lincoln, comes off as intended, but in the darkness of the gym. Enough light enters from over door windows at the south end of the gym floor that his performance is possible. Power to the school is returned. Repair is made to shorted underground lines in time for the Abe finale.

The plan to bus all the students home if power could not be restored by 10:00 A.M is deemed unnecessary due to the repair but with just a handful of minutes to spare.

Today's lunch is served as a sack-lunch of carrots and celery, peanut butter (not borrowed from the lad) and jelly, finished off with an apple for dessert. In a last minute rush

Mr. Aartemann is able to collect two to three gallons of apple cores, half-eatens, and whole undesired Jonathans to take home to feed Spot, the twins, and the rest of the deer herd that feed at his salt block location.

"They'll like the fruit addition to the whole kernel corn that is the regular fare in the baking pan turned deer feeder nailed to a log on the far side of my pond," he shares with the kitchen staff.

That is a wee positive side to the day's power outage.

On the down side yet, he is still cold. It is the end of the school day and he is nearly as chilled as he was in the morning. Students are returning home on warm busses. Staff dismissal time is here, finally, and the art room is now only up to sixty-two degrees. His toes, ankles, legs, fingers, and nose are still cold.

"We survived the outage, braved the elements, foraged for lunch but I'm yet chilled to the bone. I should make one of those 'I survived' T-shirts to remember the occasion," he mutters, but not as a happy trooper.

Heading down the hall now intentionally darkened with hallway light switches in the off position, he walks side by side with a colleague.

"This day takes the cake. Don't it beat all? I think this foolish frigidness today helped me decide on retirement. Lawyers and CEO's never have to work in these temperatures."

The colleague walks on saying nothing in response to his ranting.

"I'm out o' here! My sweetie e-mailed me after power returned and said she'd warm me up if I came home. Can't beat that offer! I'm going home! Apples too!"

Spring Eve

He carries his journal to his teacher's desk to write the urgency of words in his head. There is no assurance a moment will allow the penning but perhaps in segments at least the main thoughts can be put to ink before brain cells further age. He needs to write prior to them beginning to lose the content. The words are of memories and sightings at his home. Jottings also relate to teaching since it's an awakening of spring. His heart exits the classroom heading toward a pond like Huck Finn's need for a raft on the Mississippi.

The writing tool found quickest is a grading pencil and the words are entered into the journal with scarlet hue.

Just a few days ago they, Mr. Aartemann and Gail, witnessed a trio of wild wolves ("Are there any tame ones?" he thinks to himself as he realizes what he has written in red lead.) or coyotes passing their property just inside the edge of a wooded area next door to their house. The wolves wore gray uniforms, camouflaged into the wood's drabness, and walked in a staggered single file like a military column in search of the enemy ready to attack or defend in any direction as the need may come. It was a powerful scene, not without some fear that the animals dared come so close to the house. It was an awesome thing to get to see such a wild scene from the safety of the living room and the ruggedness of the winter woods behind the frozen pond. Winter peace broken only by the movement of the three stalkers was in its own way a beautiful thing—a wilderness of beauty.

And that too is a creation of God as surely as spring crocus, spotted fawns, a wood's litter of kittens, and fist size bunnies, he thinks to himself, and then pencils.

The ice of the pond is in the process of losing its strength with temperatures once again topping the freeze point. At night the pond is frozen. Later, afternoons present a thick, watery, slick, shiny surface shouting like a billboard that spring is near. The night freeze to afternoon thaw in February, triggers the run of maple sap at a quickened pace. Flap jacks, mush, and waffles echo spring's call, even if the preference is Mrs. Butterworths' Lite over nature's product of boiled down "tree blood."

That is the disgusting way he enjoys explaining to elementary students the origin of maple syrup. It is easy to relate human veins and blood to the veins and sap of the trees. Especially since Indiana has local sugar maples. Aartemann, the teacher, justifies that the explanation is also a good connection of art with health, nature, and science.

"I wonder how many again think upon my syrup hype as they pour the sticky sweetness on their food at breakfast." Aartemann ponders as he thinks about all of the "Ug's" and "Yuck's" and "Gross's" and "Oo-o's" that his reference to tree blood brings out of elementary students.

Just last night's melt over the top of inches of pond ice made him anxious for spring's arrival. The water and the temperature cheered him. It encouraged him to swap coats. His fake down-filled jacket is a Wal-Mart prize purchase that influenced some fellow teachers to suggest he looks a bit like the Michelin Man or the Staypuff Marshmallow Man. The replacement is a light weight cotton jacket styled in a hunter green color that he loves. He likes the lightweight aspect and color. Mostly he likes the warm air reason for the change. It is his favorite jacket when he has to wear a covering at all. It was a gift from his son and daughter-in-law. It's special.

Now that the switch to the light jacket is made, he will tomorrow be yearning for a sign that nary a jacket is needed. *It is queer how very little it takes from God, such as wetness on ice, to put me into blissful assurance of another "winterpassing,"* he thinks but does not include in this prose.

> More of a thrill was the huge; no doubt the largest, bird sighting of all he had seen in his back yard area. A blue heron landed directly in the center of the quarter inch depth of melted pond lying atop the lingering ice.

What a huge signal of inevitable spring, he thinks. *What a magnificent specimen it was,* and he writes that down.

How regal and statuesque it stood, as through at attention in the middle of a water space. It was surely proclaiming to the entire world the spot to be solely his. The heron staked his claim to the new water. It claimed all the fishing rights and all the food and all the entertainment it would for the next three seasons provide. He simply ignored Aartemann's own claim surely adequately advertised by his name visible on the mailbox at the end of the crushed limestone driveway. But that was on the front side of the house.

Another spring sign revealed itself at the same moment as the skiff of water. It was the emergence of that crushed limestone layer that has far too long been entombed under ice, sleet, packed snow and all manner of winter cold and hazard.

The heron did not stay long after filing his claim. He may have been discouraged over the icy cold under his toes. Perhaps he sensed that fishing was unproductive on this day. But he stood tall and proud, posing for a perfect Kodak moment that went un-captured. The human observers were as stock still as the heron due to the rapturous sighting.

His strength and grace and tremendous wingspan allowed a lift off into full flight that was of a beauty that can only be produced by God's creatures. A single step and a single flap of wings unfolded so smoothly that it appeared a choreographed ballet that sent him heavenward. His legs stretched flat. Wings floated rather than flapped and Mr. Heron presented the visual sensuality of flight. Off to the west like a sun at a set the heron left; a mental image, the only thing remaining as the spring omen. Not even a footprint exists for proof.

The eve of springtime flashed in the day's dawn as a single doe passed through the feeding station across the thawing pond, searching alone for food. Winter tends to herd the deer naturally and in spring the does veer off the pack to make their way alone again, and perhaps with God's help as well as stag fellows, friendly and eager, bring into the area another fawn.

Could we, Aartemann thinks to himself in a day-dreamy mood, *be so lucky to once again have a regular doe visitor bring her newly born fawn to our yard? Can we be so bold to wish a second year to watch a set of twins grow up, allowing twin sightings as often? Two each week? Nothing screams spring like a fawn so wee that it barely could reach mid thigh. Oh, if we could get so close to actually measure that way, using the knee and thigh.*

"Before a fawn will appear, the crocus come trumpeting from brown grass wet with snow melt. Will I hear them tonight? Oh spring, where art thou?"

"Mr. Aartemann, are you OK?" a student asks from a worktable.

The class has entered and sits down looking his way while he is writing and thinking so hard he misses their entry. The last of what the writer/teacher thought in his mind, he has also said aloud. He stands to address the class.

"Oh spring, where art thou? Oh spring, where art

thou? Oh spring, where art thou? Welcome class, I'm excited about spring, it's almost here, and it's Spring Eve. Would you like to do a spring project in art? (Yes!) Good, let's finish our paintings of the winter scene and next class period we will begin a spring project, promise! I can't wait. Spring Eve is here!"

Another class is underway. Aaretmenn dodges the embarrassment of talking to himself in front of his class. The sun is shining out the windows, making snow piles on the playground blacktop melt to dirty hills. Students paint and the art teacher takes his comfy swivel seat and begins anew to dream of spring. Only time will tell if he again drifts off into his own world and begins talking to himself.

"Mr. Aartemann? Mr. Aartemann? Mr. Aartemann, hel-low-ow!"

"Yes, dear." Aartemann regains conscious awareness and corrects. "Oh, it's you Abs, er, uh, Abby, er, Mrs. Sledford. Uh, what can I do for you?" and he glances to notice thankfully that the class is still working and not listening.

"Your next class is waiting in the hall. You were day dreaming. You need to switch classes. You're late," Mrs. Sledford informs him nicely, but with a smirk.

"Oh!" Aartemann jumps to his feet. "Class, put brushes in the water cup, close the paints, place your project in the drying rack and get in line. We're late! It's my fault. Please help me out. I'll clean up the paints and brushes, just put your project away and make a line. Hurry!"

Abs just steps aside and shakes her head with a

grin. Aartemann shuffles over beside her in the rush of cleanup.

"Okay, what was I saying out loud? Never mind, I gotta stop. Remember what we talked about the other day at lunch? I gotta get my resignation letter in for retirement. I have to get out of this job. I can't seem to concentrate and stay with it any longer. I'm too old. Okay, what did I say? Never mind, I need to get the paint stuff off the tables fast. Thanks for saving me."

"I'll send you a bill. Want me to help with the tables?"

"Thanks, you're an angel."

She brings the last of the supplies to the sink where he soaks brushes for a later cleaning. The next class is already nearly into the room and seated.

"This is the last of the things off the tables, take a deep breath. You're okay you know."

"Thanks again. Pray for the change, you know what change. I gotta, it's beginning to show."

Aartemann breathes deeply and pivots. "Greetings, class. Let's start today with finger exercises. Like this. One, two, one, two, one, two … good … keep it going while I pull out your drawing projects. Just like P.E. Everyone do some finger calisthenics. Now finger jumping-jacks. Now some finger stretches. One, two, one, two."

"Dear Lord, help me to the end," and he doesn't know or care if it is said mentally or verbally.

Got Mail

He stops by the workroom eating the last few bites of the apple. The peal, flesh, and color constitute all three courses of his lunch. That is, if you do not consider the preliminary rounds of coffee. And then the dessert course of more coffee. The workroom consists of machines that officially require special training before staff is allowed to touch. The copier is supposed to be fool proof but it actually has seven different places that paper, or paper facsimiles can be inserted. Three exit sites cause confusion. One is to the left and two on the right. A control panel rivals anything seen when the little door opens momentarily to the cockpit of the plane ushering teachers to warm sandy beaches for Spring Break. Topping all is a high tech unbelievable development of two lids. One is built on top of and within the other. Even having passed through the training, Aartemann has no idea what the second lid can do.

And then there is, across the room, the machine that does the same thing as the copier. Warp speed is not promised but it uses paper at least ten times faster and supposedly cheaper. They, administrators, don't seem to add those many repair costs to the total expense of printing. This machine has a permanent "out of order" sign. Occasionally it's removed when the machine is operational. It can happen, and did, at least once prior to Spring Break. Then in spring, it broke. It also has a minimum paper limit, much like some toll roads that carry a minimum speed limit. This nameless machine has a paper limit of twenty five to thirty. Minimum? X to Y is a span between numbers and not a true definitive limit according to what was taught in college when Mr. Aartemann attended. He uses this machine sparingly, as directed.

There is also a machine that looks a lot like the ironing machine in the dry cleaning work room where he has his professional cleaning done. Well, at least until he grew out of his professional clothes. The ironing look-alike sandwiches flat items of choice between two layers of clear Saran Wrap. It's not really Saran Wrap. Not like what is used to wrap up a Vidalia onion and Velveeta cheese sandwich on rye. That'll get him going! Saran is another Aartemann pet peeve. The machine wrap clings together to itself just as good as the Saran Wrap does when you try to get the roll started the first time the box is opened. It also mimics the store bought wraps by not clinging to the items being preserved. Failure happens at least half the time. He calls it the Saran Lamentationer and avoids its use.

There is a non-motorized (an awesome concept) device called an Ellison something-or-other but has nothing to do with lighting or outdated technological audio equipment. The art man mistakes lots of names. Edison for Ellison. Ellison makes letters. It punches out four-inch tall letters from construction paper, one at a time. Or it makes five-inch capitals at the same speed that human hands can change paper and pull a lever. The lever arm reminds Las Vegas Spring Break vacationers of losses.

Teachers think of Spring Break a lot between Christmas and Memorial Day.

Between the double lidded and the Las Vegas arm stands a folding table that holds a wooden set of cubby holes known locally as the mail boxes. Aartemann uses today's lunchtime, passing by the workroom, to check for mail. Got mail!

Legal size envelopes are stacked to one side. Last week he'd found a Dumdums sucker in his box. Everybody got one for a treat from someone. His was crème soda, his favorite Dumdums flavor. He didn't even have to trade it with one in another mailbox. He would do that without guilt, when no one is around. For he likes his crème soda flavor.

First opening is a thick envelope. It is a multi-page information bulletin that gives directions about the insurance plan. It is too small a type to read without his glasses and they are still on the keyboard at his desk. Another senior moment! Insurance thinking is stress-thinking most of the time for someone who makes a living with pictures. So the stapled stack that gives a mental impression of volumes is again enveloped. Something like ... nobody opts for a toothache.

Back at the desk, he finishes his apple down to the slimmest core. It is a Granny Smith and the sour white inside begins taking on pink spots. Usually slowly munching a Granny Smith will allow the appearance of browning, but not pink. Suddenly he realizes he has bit his lip somewhere in the dining process. Lip blood is mixing with apple juice. Each bite now adds another pink splotch. He tries to eat around his own blood loss. Finally he tosses the core into the basket beside the desk completing the solid portion of lunch. He probably should call the custodian for assistance with disposing of the core through the hazardous fluid spill procedure.

He opens the next envelope.

> McArdman (The r in Mr. had a leading right tail making it look like a c.) I like to PaintI really Like Do it when we paint eD the houses. (The small k's in the 'like' words looked like capital N's.)
>
> —Beth Wevre

That letter looks something like a classroom writing assignment which prompted thanking a teacher. He opens the next envelope.

> Dear Mr. Aartemann,
> I like the drawing skills that you taught me. Some that I remember and use are: one square at time, shading, making trees, T square and many more. They were hard when you first taught me, but now they are simple. I did not know how to draw the first year I came to your class. Now I put all the drawing skills together and draw animals, people, and mostly cars. I hope that one of my best drawings with the skills you tought me would go in a museum in New York.
> Yours truly,
> Brad Alexander

One final envelope is torn open.

> Dear Mr. Aartemann,
> Thanks for all your help in art class. Especialy when I had troble with the one square at a time. I also liked the Victorian house project. Then it got put in the

festival. Thank's for all your halp Mr. Aartemann.

These are the reasons you are my favorite art teacher.

Sincerely,

John Bronkmar.

Aartemann is John's only art teacher.

Aartemann prays softly to himself, "Okay, God, it's just three very tiny reasons for not retiring, but I see the point. It just confuses the decision. Now clear my confusion, please."

Spring Break

"Hi, woman! You're here on time for a change. That's unusual, what happened, did your clock stop? You had to guess, right? Accidentally arrived early, right? Or were you out with that guy, what's his name, the one you were taking to the concert?"

"You curmudgeon, sit down," the counselor orders.

"You're not the boss of me," Aartemann responds to Abs.

Still he sits for a spell in her office holding his thermos on his lap. A black soft sided briefcase is set on the floor. It flops over spilling pencils.

"Now look what you caused. Great help you are. How is that 'ro-man-s-s-ee' goin'?"

He stretched the words out emphasizing syllables that didn't exist.

"So give me the sexy, oops I mean, gory details. You still seeing him? I haven't heard much from you lately, what's the scoop?"

She turns after putting items away in a file drawer and displays an un-rested face.

"Whoa, you okay? Sorry, but you don't look so good. You need coffee? I have some, no crème and sugar, but I'm not sure you need that right now. What's up? Spring break is around the corner and you look worse than I feel."

He is honest but not very sympathetic. It is their way. They get to the point with each other fast.

"It's already been a long day and it will get longer. There was an accident over the weeken …"

The school intercom activates and the announcement begins.

"Attention staff!"

It is the principal and he is earlier than normal too. Something is going on. Something happened.

"Many of you already know of the automobile accident over the weekend involving one of our families. Jeremy Cross, in Dorothy Best's first grade class, was relatively unhurt. His brother, Nate McDonald of Janet Neuenschwander's fifth grade is now in good condition in the hospital. Their mother and her companion were killed. The children will not be in school this week and we will let you know of plans after next week's Spring Break vacation. There will be a number of guests here this morning from other schools and area churches to assist students with concerns or problems. Call the office if help is needed. The first and fifth grades will each have a grade level meeting with a counselor leading. It will begin immediately after the opening bell. The recommendation, as always, is simply try to make it as normal a day as possible. Address individual students' needs as they occur.

"The funeral arrangements are being sent to your desktop. Coverage will be provided for any staff that would like to attend the service on Wednesday. Thank you."

"Oh my! Sorry, Abs, I stuck my foot in mouth again. You okay?"

"Yes! The principal and I spent the morning helping round up someone to watch Nate till family could arrive later today. They've only been in our district for a bit over a year. All other family is out of state. They don't seem to have been a church family so there was no help there. It's pretty sad. The man that lived with them was not either of the boys' real dads. We don't know where they are at this point, likely another state as well. A different dad for each sibling is not that uncommon any more. I'll take some of that coffee you offered."

He pours into her cup and she adds sweetener from a packet in her desk drawer.

"This could be a long day," they both say in unison. "You owe me a coke!" they both reply, again in unison.

It's a phrase from their youth lost to today's generation. They laugh and the gloom is temporarily broken.

"He's great!"

"Who?"

"You curmudgeon! Paul, the gentleman that I took to the concert. You wouldn't understand … gentleman, I mean. And then he took me out to eat. (She sticks her nose in the air while she speaks.) You wouldn't know about nice things like that 'cause you're a curmudgeon."

The banter is back—something of normalcy.

"Oh, you never told me your knight in shining armor's name. Paul, huh? So is Paul a regular thing? How far away does he live again? What did he feed you, hot wings? Is he macho? You need macho. Are you going to see him during Spring …"

The principal sticks his head in the door.

"Come to my office, Abby, as soon as you can."

And he was off.

"Well I need to go and get ready for classes. I can't quite picture Jeremy yet. He must be a quiet one. I think

I have his class today. I know I have Neuenschwander's fifth grade later. I know Nate. He's quiet too. He's the one that seldom finishes and seldom works. One time, drawing a dog, he loves dogs; he did a marvelous colored pencil thing. I put it on display on the cupboard door right over his work table and he spent the next two art class periods staring at his own drawing. He was very pleased, I think. Because it was hanging up. He gets little work hung up. I need to get him more dogs to draw. That is, if he is ever back in this school. Rough life for some of these kids. It just doesn't seem fair, does it? Well, good luck today. Come see me at lunch. We'll do coffee. I want to hear more about Paul. I need to make sure he's good enough for you."

"And I need to know about your retirement plans. You do deserve to get to do that, you know?"

"Yeh, yeh. For that I could kiss you bye but you have coffee breath." and he was off.

"Hi. How did it go? Did you have a lot of students to deal with due to the accident?"

Aartemann motions for counselor Abby to sit at a small table beside his desk as he pushes aside stacks of ungraded and undisplayed completed art assignments. He has been working on word-processing some of the writing that the students completed about their project. They often write about the project's success or difficulty when they finish early. It fills the time when they finish ahead of the other class members. It also reinforces writing draft skills.

"Is that all you're eating?" she asks looking directly at the oversized Granny Smith apple half eaten in his hand.

"It is unless you brought me pie and ice cream."

"All I have is these rice cakes. Want one?"

"No thanks, I have my own Styrofoam in the crafts cupboard over there."

"Curmudgeon!"

"So—o?"

"It went well this morning in first and fifth. The students are resilient. You were right, the boys are both very quiet and loners. Since they are newcomers to our area they have neither local family nor many close friends. Actually, they seem to have almost no friends at all. It's really a bit sad."

"I didn't notice a thing when Mrs. Best's first grade came to art. They didn't even mention the meeting or Jeremy. It was business as usual. Yeh, kinda sad isn't it?"

"So, you are retiring at the end of the year aren't you?"

"Wrong topic. It didn't work. Paul who? What's this farmer's last name? Does he have a last name?"

"Paul Williams. He's not a farmer, he's a ... oh, you curmudgeon, you knew that. He's sensitive. I'll ask him to come and visit you so you can have a lesson."

"Ooo, so he's invited back. Sounds serious. Did you kiss? Okay, really, is it working? You goin' to go see him?"

"Yes. But don't tell anyone here. I'm not real comfortable with that yet. We're meeting in Phoenix at a resort for four days during spring break next week."

"Nice! You having separate roo ... oh, never mind, not my business. Doesn't matter, that's your business. Gonna golf? It's expensive out there."

"Yes. And yes."

"Huh?"

"Yes, separate rooms, you know me better than that. Yes, golf. And yes expensive but we get a free round with our amenities at the resort, with a cart. Well not free, the rooms are $238.00 a night."

"Big spender! This is serious."

"It really is. I've never been happier. This is really *big*!"

She shouts the word big and Miss Cable, the librarian, stops suddenly in the hallway while walking by the art room. Understandably, she looks in their direction.

"Now you've done it. You aroused the interest of Miss Cable. What she doesn't know she can make up and the gossip mill begins with Cable. You know that. All she knows is you and I eat together. She probably assumes it is a daily occurrence, and you're shouting superlatives, and my wife's gonna kill me. Big huh? Okay, give me juicy details. Was he in your hot tub yet? You taking a swim suit to Phoenix? Bikini? Never mind, you'll probably wear one of those three piece things, two layers, with a skirt that covers your knees. Good luck with Paul, you being in a Victorian queen costume like that."

"Curmudgeon!"

"Can't you come up with a four letter word to call me? Paul, Paul Williams? Isn't he a TV celebrity or movie star or an author or something? Is that who you're sinking your fangs into? Sorry, we have to end this little date. Some of us have to work. I have a class in just a few minutes and nothing is on the tables yet. Glad your day's better, you look better too. I know—Paul!"

"Retirement?"

"Probably. We're going to try to decide over spring break for sure. I may wait to decide during the summer. I know that would cause me to give up the severance and early retirement incentives. For me that amounts to little anyhow. I don't want a big sendoff. I hate things like that. The scales really lean to retirement. For sure—almost! Please don't tell anyone. Besides I can retract a retirement plan letter up until the end of July."

"I won't mention your retirement if you forget to mention Paul."

"Deal."

"Deal."

They shake.

The fourth grade class begins entering the art room as Aartemenn pulls the projects folder from the storage bin. He hands the papers for distribution to a pair of students as they enter. They know the routine. The smiles on their two faces show how little it takes to make their day. Aartemann covets.

Aartemann dreams of his own smiles on the patio on the first day of school next year.

Tim Lantz slides sideways into the art room door and glances off the jamb, ricocheting back into the hall. Kedric Trout, at a run, jumps into the entry while watching Tim's bounce. He squares immediately to march straight into the art studio. Aartemann steps sideways from behind the cupboard bin stack and directly into young Trout's path. Aartemann's step goes unnoticed. Kedric makes his sudden collision stop with his face sideways on the chest of Mr. Aartemann. In total surprise, Kedric looks up into the teacher's face. Aartemann has his eyes opened as wide as humanly possible. He's intentionally holding his breath to cause facial redness. Eyebrows are arched so high they form an almost half circle. A circle is the shape of his gasping mouth expression.

"Oops, sorry!" Kedric emits as he attempts a side step around the body of Aartemann.

But the barricade body steps in front of him again. There is a repeat of the collision.

"Wait," is all that Mr. Aartemann says.

Tim finally enters the room having seen Kedric's mistake. Aartemann uses one finger to suggest Tim's joining their location. He lowers his head and complies.

"Well?" Aartemann queries as both boys face his stare.

Contorted face skin is part of a severe look Mr. Aartemann can give that just screams "deep doo-doo time."

"He pushed me."

Tim speaks first hoping to pass the blame.

"He kicked me first."

Kedric verbally retaliates and passes the baton.

"Tim, you forgot to mention your kicking," Aartemann reminds.

"He ran and broke in front of me," Tim fortifies his defense.

"That's because you pulled my shirt out."

"Cause you were running."

"You too."

"You first."

"Whoa, soldiers. Let me get this straight," Aartemann begins. "You were running, and then you were running, and then you pulled his shirt out ..."

"On accident!" Tim supplied, like it should make a difference.

"Sh—h! You were running, and then you were running, and then you pulled his shirt, and then you kicked, and you broke in line, and then you pushed, and then you threw a rock, and then you pointed a knife, and then you swung an axe, and then you drew a gun, and then you threw a grenade, and then you dropped a bomb, and then you sent the army, and then you got the British Navy on your side, and then you ..."

By this time the room is silent and the whole class is listening. The offenders are wide eyed and about to smirk at Aartemann's rambling story. Yet they are terribly afraid at what might happen if they do.

"You two just about started world war three because both of you were running in the hall. It's not nice to run in the hall. It is not the procedure to run in the hall. How should you go down the hall?"

"Walk."

The pair speak the word simultaneously. Aartemann almost laughs, not from their predicament, but from the memory of he and Abs doing the same thing earlier in the day.

You owe him a Coke! Aartemann wants to say, but he does not.

"Right, soldiers, walk! Now walk to your seat. Get to work. Don't ever let me catch you running and pushing in the hall again. Okay?"

"Yes."

"Yes, Mr. Aartemann."

The class gets to work. Ample snickering and whispering occur throughout the room. A lesson is learned by all. This time with no blood shed.

"Now I hope you see why they call these three colors the primary colors. So if you want to go to the store like Wal-Mart, or K-Mart, or Z-Mart, or Whirly-gig Mart, or any store and buy paint for a picture of Noah and the Ark with a rainbow but you only have three dollars and each color of paint costs one dollar a bottle and … Beth, how many bottles of paint can you buy for your three dollars? This sounds like a math lesson instead of art, doesn't it?"

"Three!" she proudly answers Mr. Aartemann's question.

Four hands go up to give their own answer. A couple are likely to correct what they believe is Beth's mistake.

"Right. What you need to know is that if you buy the three primary colors … what are they, class?"

"Red, yellow and blue," is the almost unison answer. Only one trailing answer ends in something sounding like the letter n.

"Right again. Red, yellow, and blue; the three primary colors are the beginning colors. All other colors come from those three colors. Well, it works with light colors, anyway. You see, color is really the light reflected off objects. Your eyes see colors because of the light rays. At least for most people, some people are color blind. They see but only in black and white and grays."

He sees he is beginning to loose some of the students with the scientific aspect of color.

"Okay, it's like this. If we had three spotlights, and had color filters to color the light coming out of each of them, one red, one blue, and one yellow; then we could shine the three colored spots on the wall. What color do you think you would see?" he asked.

"Black"

"Brown"

"Pouy-pal" is a response from a second grader with a speech defect. Every student seems to have an answer. All are offering color names at the same time. Mr. Aartemann holds up his hand with the index finger and thumb extended into an L letter signaling the class to listen.

"You would actually see white. White is the presence of all color. Since the three primary colors are the beginning colors that all other colors are made from; then shining the lights on the same spot on the wall would produce a white light. Really!" he added seeing skepticism in several students.

They usually believe anything he comes up with as the gospel.

"Now black is the absence of all color. That means anything you view as a black color is not reflecting light rays. If we turn out all of the lights in the room, what would we see? Blackness. (It was rhetorical; he didn't wait for any answer.) Has anyone ever been inside of a cave when they turned all of the lights out?"

Three hands go up. In a second grade class there is always a student or two that will claim to have seen, have done, have owned, or have eaten anything mentioned. Some are especially responsive if it makes them the only one with the experience. It has something to do with an eight year's old need for fame.

"What did you see?"

"Nothing," Sam replies.

Sam's a student that likely did visit a cave with his family at some time.

"Right on!" Aartemann cheers. "You can't even see your hand about to touch your face in complete darkness. It's like being blind. Oops, sorry!"

He has been tossing a half stick of chalk up and down in one hand while he lectured the students. The chalk went astray and landed with a bounce off of the head of Janet Ornby sitting right in front of where he stood. She began giggling so hard that she slipped off her chair to her knees. A full minute or two is required for her to get composed, along with the majority of the rest of the class as well. Laughter is as contagious in a second grade group as barfing.

"Mixing two primary colors together gives us second-ary colors. Each one has its own name. What do we get when we mix primary yellow with primary red?" he asks Janet.

"Orange," she answers and immediately goes into another spell of giggles.

Echoes of giggles by a smaller number of other students follow.

"What do we get if we mix primary yellow with primary blue? It is a secondary color. What is its name?" pointing to Brooke.

"Green?" she offers questioningly.

"Yes, it is green," and he places letters on the board in appropriate places.

The letter locations are heading in the direction of a color wheel.

"And the last secondary comes from mixing primary blue with primary red and it is called … ?"

After pointing to Benjamin, not Ben (just ask, he'll tell you), he answers, "Purple."

Aartemann writes a "V" on the board. Ben immediately changes his answer to Violet. Aartemann immediately erases the V and makes a P causing Ben to change again back to purple. The art teacher teases by changing once again back to a V.

"Actually, this color has two names. Violet and purple are the same color. On your Crayola crayon, they even put both names on the wrapper."

He continues, "So, the light gives us all of the colors. The light that shines through the raindrops gives us a rainbow against the sky. Rainbows have all of the colors separated from the white light that is the presence of all color. The sunshine is needed for the rainbow. God made the sun. God made the moon and stars and He is known as The Light of the World. The rainbow is His gift to us and it is a sign of His promise and commitment to us in this world. The base of the rainbow begins with purple or violet, then blue, then green, then all of the colors in order. God made the order. Perhaps the base of violet signifies His royalty, as He is the King of Kings, the Lord of Lords, and the Prince of Peace. In Genesis, the Bible says: 'Whenever the rainbow appears in the clouds, I will see it and remember the everlasting covenant between God and all living creatures of every kind on the earth.'"

Mr. Aartemann began pounding on the table like a revival preacher commanding the attention of the second grade congregation. The pounding continued until he startles alert. He rolls his head to the side. He reads the green clock numbers. It is 5:57 A.M He has been beating the mattress with his fist. Memory finally recalls his teaching or preaching a color lesson to the second grade. The alarm has not been set but his inner alarm goes off only two minutes late from a normal day. He ignores the clock. He shakes the dream off while fluffing his pillow, and closes his eyes.

He walks around the room, selecting students to answer to what would be made from color mixes.

He says "red and yellow," points, and the students follow with a reply.

"Blue and red?"

"Violet."

"Blue and yellow?"

"Green."

"Blue and green?"

"Brown?"

"No, nice try. Blue green is the color name from primary blue and secondary green. They say the primary color first. Okay? Now try … orange and red?"

"Red orange."

"Good, you said the primary color first. Purple and Red?"

"Red purple?"

"No, it's really called red violet because … well I don't know why. I think red purple should be OK too, but it's not. Somebody made up the names and didn't ask me. So we'll have to call it red violet. Now, yellow and orange?"

"Yellow orange," the students are not even raising hands any longer and all want to give the answers.

Mass response shows the entire group seems to have a good grasp on color mixing on the color wheel. Aartemann also has explained to them that he was not asked what to call the color wheel when it was invented, just like the red violet name. He thinks color circle would be just as good. Or he likes color donut, and color ring, but again, he was not asked even though he told the kids that he thought he is old enough to have probably been alive when they invented the wheel. That statement the second graders believe.

"Green and yellow?"

He looks at the clock again in a daze. Aloud he speaks, "Yellow green" as he reads the yellow green numbers now reporting 6:02 A.M He awakes enough to realize he went right back to sleep continuing to dream about teaching the second grade art color lesson. The religion aspect was eliminated over the past five minutes of dream.

Why do I have to dream of work? he asks himself, this time silently, hoping the yellow green statement has not awakened his wife. She had gone to bed earlier than him due to a cold. It is still dark. Only a hint of light is observable, *like the gloaming of Scotland,* he thinks. He wants to go back to sleep but without dreaming. He lays still and prays for his wife's cold. Stillness lets him go back to sleep and to the vacation plans.

"Vacation plans!" he almost shouts it. Inwardly he does. He realizes for the first time that he is on vacation. There is no need to wake up at any particular time. The alarm is not set. They can sleep in late. Why is he awake? They will travel by plane out to the southwest but that is not for five days yet. He rolls to his right side and closes his eyes another time.

Students are at a peak of excitement, it seems, with school confinement. When a vacation is looming, they sense it like perfume in the air. It tends to make more than a few of them a bit destructive or distractive.

"Joel, that is not the normal procedure for a student

here in our four star school. What exactly should that eraser be used for? Have you any idea?"

Duh, I donno, is the response though not verbal. It is suggested with the shrug of the shoulders. Joel is staring at the edge of the table.

"Please look at me and tell me what an eraser is best used for."

"Erasing?" Joel answers this time. Still there is no eye contact.

"Correct, very good. Now, why are you throwing erasers instead of the erasing that you know is what they are for?"

Shrug. Eyes aimed at the floor.

"Keenan, do you think you would like someone putting an extra marker line on your drawing?"

Shrug.

"Keenan, do you think you would like someone drawing on your project?"

Shrug.

"Keenan, can I mark all over your picture?"

"No." Keenan finally finds some vocabulary.

"Why shouldn't we be allowed to mark on your pictures if you think you are allowed to mark on pictures of the people that work at your table? Do you think you should have privileges that we do not have? Ever hear of Leonardo? (A nod.) Do not try to mark on one of his paintings because the police will put you in jail, or maybe shoot you. And who knows, maybe somebody in here will be as famous as Leonardo some day with his or her painting."

"I thought Leonardo was a Mutant Ninja Turtle," Keenan half whispers.

Aartemann shakes his head, rolls his eyes, and thinks unprofessionally as he returns to his desk to sit, *I need a vacation.*

In another class a lad is deliberately breaking the lead of colored pencils. Then he runs to the pencil sharpener with three or four at a time. If another is already using the sharpener he is pushing or poking. Mr. Aartemann, stops him. Aartemann removes him from the worktable. He puts away his project. Professor Aartemann returns to his swivel teacher seat allowing the boy to live.

"Misty, take the marker out of your mouth. You should see what your lips and mouth look like now. (She tried to hide her face.) What will you tell your mom when you get home and your mouth is four different colors? Do you think anyone wants to use that marker after you have slobbered all over it? Not me! Wipe your mouth with a paper towel and wipe off the markers also. Oh well, it's not working, the color's still on your lips."

With that final statement he heads to sit down. Misty grabs another paper towel and just about rubs her lips to the gum line.

"Mr. Aartemann? Can I get a drink?"

"No, there is only three minutes left. Besides, I'm out of coffee and if I can't drink something then you can't drink."

"I don't want to be here!"

"I don't want to be here either," agrees Luke who sits closest to the teacher desk and overhears the teacher's remark.

He shakes off the next awakening at 6:33 A.M with

great effort. It seems almost useless to try to sleep. He is trying to awake from the inside out. His desire is a spring vacation first day sleep in. The school day auto alarm apparently implanted by monster alien forces will not comply. He slept poorly, unless sleeping with school classroom nightmares is considered desirable.

Nearly 7:00 A.M he sees looking with just one eye because using both eyes seems to blur the clock. He lays awake, thinking of writing or reading. Either will require getting out of bed without waking her. He tries counting sheep instead of students and that silly sleep method actually works.

At 7:19 A.M she crawls out with great care making sure to avoid waking her husband, the art teacher, on his first day of spring break. He is awake with his eyelids closed having been awakened at a sound she'd made. An "Ugh!" He feigns sleep and peeks out one eye when he hears her head toward the door. She begins to slowly close the by-fold doors to the bedroom. She seems okay, at least better. She is heading for the hot pot to make her first cup of tea. Mrs. Aartemann starts every day with a tea, Lipton or Tazo. She likely will begin a pot of coffee for him as well. That is the routine.

Mr. Aartemann prays again for concerns coming to mind but as always, first for his wife. He drifts again to sleep during the prayer. With dreams of school yet relentless, he awakes again after a twenty minute interval of horizontal unfruitful sleep. He realizes he has been talking to the other teachers, teachers from his last dream. The dream location is at his school and he talked in the dream about his earlier dreams of school.

"Oh my, I guess it's time to get up. Now I'm dreaming about dreaming about school. Or I've gone nuts, loony, ready for the funny farm! I need coffee."

He thinks the thoughts, or says them aloud; he doesn't know which. Maybe he is dreaming that too.

He crawls out of bed, finally becoming alert. Even with his recovered consciousness it seems so much like a normal Saturday of a weekend between school weeks. But it is Friday! It is the first day of spring break. Break consists of a total of nine days since it begins with a day off on Friday. He will not be required to teach again till a week from Monday. He stretches and smiles and smells Starbucks Sumatra.

"Ah," he says aloud to himself but loud enough for her to hear in the kitchen. "It seems like Saturday which is great because that gives me a bonus day of vacation in my head. What a night."

Then he thinks about this day being Friday. That gives him another day of vacation. Then he remembers dreaming about school and about dreaming about telling fellow teachers about dreaming. He is not sure he should be telling anyone, even his wife, about how his brain is operating right at this moment.

He whispers to himself, "Perhaps I *need* this vacation worse than I thought. Is this dream an omen for the week? I'll talk to and ask Abs, the school counselor—tonight— in a dream, since she is headed to Phoenix for her own spring break vacation."

He laughs at himself making Mrs. Aartemann wonder what is going on.

"Want me to make biscuits?" he asks Gail.

They work at it together. When baking is complete they sit in a wide oversize chair with a plate of the biscuits, a tub of butter for dipping, her tea, and his coffee. They bless it and ask for peace and rest through the vacation time, even in the travel to come in a few days. While eating he fills her in on his night of dreams. He usually forgets them right away, but not this time. When he finishes, he kisses her. She tastes of butter.

Then he also remembers his dream on the last school night, the eve prior to Christmas vacation's beginning. He just doesn't seem to do vacation starts very well. He dreamed about school, a really weird dream, at that time also. Perhaps he has a nocturnal separation anxiety thing about leaving school for a vacation. He'd really like to know if this happens to other teachers—dreaming about school on the eve of a school break. But he will not ask. He is likely odd. Very odd. It will be just another thing never to live down as the art teacher.

Alarm

Arriving at school is uneventful. Arriving is routine. Arriving is just what is necessary to get on with whatever will be happening during the educational day. It will likely become somehow eventful, somehow out of routine, and always more than expected. It is just the way a teacher's day is to be. It is an ordained thing, like darkness at night, jelly on peanut butter, and a dead camera battery when a grandchild smiles and holds the perfect pose.

About as routine as the road travel from home to school is the short walking trip from the teacher parking site to the entry door always used by Mr. Aartemann. He is so predictable that other teachers even leave a particular parking space open for his vehicle. He normally arrives within a five minute time period. Aartemann always takes the same spot even though they are not assigned in any way. An official exception is the principal's parking space, which is in an entirely different location. No one knows how long he has used the same spot. Oil stains on the pavement segment memorialize signs of vehicle problems as accurately as the rings found in the smooth cut of the top of a stump show its age. His personal history could be mapped out with the oil rings on asphalt as well as coffee stains. They come from the last of his travel mug being dumped on the pavement just prior to exiting the truck or car. It is usually a truck, unless a new oil spot announces a new problem for the shop to solve.

"What's wrong with it?" the maintenance manager always asks.

"I was hoping since you are the Ford repair man and I am a teacher who knows crayons … well, I figured I'd try and let you figure it out. It is what I pay for, right?"

He always gives the staff at Clooney Ford a hard time, even though they give him fine service. He treats his chiropractor the same. But with her, it is fed right back in equal portion.

Today, arrival is routine but the minute he steps from the truck and places a foot on the yet wet pavement, he notices the difference. His eyes focus within themselves, almost as though they become conscious of the environment. All of his senses are on alert.

Notice, the senses scream inwardly and in unison.

The spring rain overnight has left the ground warmer than most days in this early part of spring. The ground being wetter than it had been also attributes to the cleanness of the smell. Overpowering the clean smell is an earthworm odor that is like perfume to Aartemann. It is the first day he has noticed the smell since last fall tumbled into winter and made smelling a frigid thing; especially if gulped. He sucks through his nostrils. Over and over he gulps air and aroma like a fisherman on Cape Cod smelling for ocean fish. The smell is a delight for Aartemann. It's almost so grand he can taste it, if one can get by the image of tasting earthworms.

Beside his awareness of the freshness of spring is the sound of the birds. Flying fowl are plentiful perhaps because of the hundreds of thousands of earthworms on the surface of the walks, parking lot, and grassy areas. They seem to be doing a chuckling sound instead of the traditional chirping on a day like this one. They are happy to see a favorite food source emerging once again.

"Sure, laugh, you ornery little birdie. I wouldn't laugh at you if you had to go to work and I got to spend the day outside. So why do you mock me? You should be ashamed."

At least this day the art teacher is talking to the birds instead of his routine of talking to himself as he enters the school building. He is alone. He always tries to remember to check that first prior to talking to himself. But he doesn't check to see if anyone is listening when he talks to the birds. He just gets lucky.

He takes one last gulp of spring freshness scrambled with the scent of night crawler slime. Grudgingly he pulls the handle of the entry.

"Save some for me," is his final plea to the birds. Since no one hears, no one has to decide if he means the sweet clean air or the shiny worm abundance.

School happens. Some is routine, but little. Elementary school and routine go together about as well as snowmen and sparklers.

It is a frantic afternoon created by an art instructor trying to instruct classes. Additionally he tries to word process hand written pages created by students writing about their visual projects, mount art pictures after the grading and recording steps, hang certain pieces in the room and hallway, set aside an assortment of art projects for hanging next week in the local city-county library, read and respond to e-mails from home and other school staff, write a journal entry, drink coffee from a stainless steel thermos, prepare for tomorrow's two morning classes (the afternoon pre-cancelled for teacher training meetings), pick up the stack of pictures that just fell off the bookshelf, gather the "stuff" needed in this day's after school arts festival organizational meeting, cut bookmarks from scrap for the school library, clean spectacles, mount student projects (mentioned already), unstop the Elmer's glue bottle for a first grader (Why don't they close those up after use so they don't crust over?), sneak down the hall to pee (Why does he drink so much coffee?), finish the nine weeks grade report, stand and stare down the student that just tossed an eraser to another work table, exhale, un-jamb the pencil sharpener, fill the water cups for the next class's watercolor session, tote that barge and lift that bale.

Nothing really changes with the next class session other than it will be third graders instead of first graders. The unstopped glue bottle remains unstopped for at least two hours. Oh yes, the coffee pot empties but the urinal need increases relatively.

When the final class of the afternoon exits, tasks begin to be completed and checked off today's to-do list. He puts things in place, materials and instructional examples, ready for the morning's first class. Lines of students from classrooms file past the art room door. Two abreast they head for the bus exit and school day's end.

He rushes the last of the grade reports to the appropriate location taking the necessary just-in-time restroom break along the way—fully forty-five minutes past extreme need.

Ten minutes after the teacher day ends and five minutes after he should be leaving for the after school meeting he is to attend ten miles away, he places a bid on eBay for a pair of books. With only twenty-one seconds to spare the bid wins. The computer is quickly shut down leaving payment for an evening chore at home.

Aartemann begins grabbing the items he needs to take with him. He notices Abs walking by the art room door looking as frazzled as he feels. He has been so busy the past week or so that they have not met.

"Abby?" he beckons.

She stops and turns with a look of "What, I'm busy" and eyes worn.

"Paul?" Aartemann questions as briefly as possible still picking up items.

Abs face brightens, eyes twinkle, and mouth corners curl up. Both arms are instantly raised with two thumbs up. They are really, really up. She silently moves on.

The light switch is located on a hall wall four feet off the floor. Its height makes it almost unreachable with one hand holding meeting paperwork, a soft side briefcase, the aforementioned thermos lightened of its fluid and the opposite hand gripping a paper Handy's Grocery bag containing no less than fourteen books for home transport. It is not pretty, but a stroke of genius, to think of flipping the switch with a right elbow averting the potential of spilled packages. Because the switch is on the left wall of the hallway, a spin, full circle, is necessary after the darkening maneuver is completed. At the flag pole exit door, another spin is used in reverse direction for backing out of the panic bar door with the full arm loads. This door opens nearest the staff parking area. The glass door has a panic bar latch which can be activated with a rump. Aartemann reaches the outside with his load. Only the vehicle's door is a last barricade till he can shed some of the weight his arms are toting. It is a weight that should have required two trips. His arms are weakening and strained.

The pickup truck door handle being nearly the same height as the light switch in the hall poses less of a threat than anticipated, during Aartemann's parking lot crossing. He opens the door with caution, as there is too little space to let the truck door open fully and freely. Care is taken so the door does not hit the gray car parked in the adjacent space. He steps up and hops into the driver seat, jockeying all packages, carrying containers and papers in a way as not to drop, spill, dump, tear or alter any of the grasped items. He must not bump the truck door further ajar, allowing it to contact that gray car sitting next to his truck. No doubt it belongs to another teacher, since most support staff leaves earlier in the day.

The bag of books, feeling now twice as heavy as when first picked up is easiest to set to a rest in the passenger side of the split bench seat. The seat is divided by a plop-down divider arm rest with cup holder still holding the morning's stainless travel mug. The mug is empty but its added height causes it to make the lift of the bag filled with fourteen books an arm strength test. Lifting the bag of books over the mug is a Herculean task even Arnold Schwrtz-his-name would struggle with.

The stainless travel mug that held the morning Star-bucks brew is decorated with The Prayer of Jabez in calligraphy. It is exactly like the matching mug in Aartemann's room. I Chronicles 4:10, "Oh that you would bless me indeed, and enlarge my territory, that your hand would be with me, and that you would keep me from evil, that I may not cause pain. So God granted him what he requested."

Aartemann had found the cups, four matching, in an old bookstore and bought them for a buck each. Today instead of the Jabez prayer, he should have prayed for additional bicep strength. He did not. The stainless cup helps none. It is an obstacle.

Beep, beep, beep, beep, beep, beep, sounds the truck's theft alarm.

Pound, pound, pound, pound, takes off his heart caused by the suddenness and volume of the alarm noise. His brain shakes as violently as his hand holding the key ring. The ring that came with the truck includes a remote unlock button directly above the alarm button. He's done this silly "oops" before. Holding yet the thermos, the soft attaché now weighing somewhat like a full duffle bag, the papers and all of it held high above the steering wheel, he maneuvers gracelessly. He is trying to access the remote. He frantically tries reaching for the door. It requires a cross-armed fashion move to stop the alarm. He suddenly remembers the gray car next to him and his open truck door.

"Rats, I must have hit the other car," then in a split second decision, *no, it's my own alarm*, he thinks. Quivering fingers fumble with his remote. He successfully touches the red button to get the alarm to silence. Instead of the anticipated quiet, the alarm multiplies.

Bee-beep, bee-beep, bee-beep, it blasts away. Two alarms now synchronized, equally loud, equal in tone, attack ears like artillery in battle. Alarms are keeping now in sync with each other and with his new heart rhythm. Natural rhythm has fallen into line with the vehicles' blasts.

Bee-beep-pound,   bee-beep-pound,   bee-beep-pound, bee-beep-pound.

"Are you awake yet?"

The female voice call comes, amid sounds of car alarm, truck alarm and vocal arrhythmia.

Hour-long seconds of time elapse. The reality of the situation begins registering to more advanced brain cells, overcoming current "fright or flight" brain stem reaction currently in control of his processes.

I just turned on my own alarm trying to turn it off, is the thought flashing through Aartemann's head. In the new haste to turn it off (or the trembling from fright) the finger shakes twice. The alarm goes off for one beep and then right back on. He punches it again, this time only once, and half the noise is gone. Within a couple of seconds more, the teacher crossing the lot toward the gray, bellowing auto finds her own button. This ends the alarm that had first been activated, starting the whole of the frantic emergency.

"Are you awake now?" she repeats and laughs.

She laughs at herself. Aartemann is still shaking too much to laugh.

"I accidentally hit the alarm on my keys. Sorry."

"I thought I'd set it off hitting it with my door. I tried to be careful. Actually I thought it was my truck alarm at first and when I tried to turn it off ... well ... that's when I turned my own truck alarm *on*. At least I'll not fall asleep on the way to my meeting."

The heart rate is returning to normal. All the gear is stowed. As the truck takes the lead leaving the school parking lot, only the audio book tape is heard. Even that noise he turns down a half a turn for good measure.

The day seems to be ending as void of routine as it began. He remembers the sweet clean smelling air and the worms. His mind flashes through the day. It has been a busy one.

"Ah, another day nearer the weekend," he muses, pushing the gas with a quake less foot. "An' summer's a comin.' Will I survive till retirement?"

No one but Aartemann and the radio is listening.

Teacher of the Year

"Hi, I've needed to see you," is the opening line from Principal Gene.

He takes his long steps toward the desk where Aartemann stands just about to grab the thermos and bag of papers in the ritual movement toward home. It is already ten minutes past clock-out time. Most teachers never leave at clock-out time nor do many arrive very close to clock-in time. Most teachers spend hours after school and extra hours before the day's official start doing what good teachers do. And they do it free. Some carry home the work and assign themselves much homework so they can at least be with their family while they work. Some use wheeled carryon luggage for the job. Most parents have not one clue of the extra hours donated.

"Heard anything new?" he questions as Aartemann notably looks a bit odd.

It is he who is on the committee proposing new alignment of staff positions for the following year. Gene is one of two administrative members, and he is this school's administrator, and with that the tired art teacher assumes he will know more than himself.

"No, I thought you might have. Nothing new?" Aartemann asks in return.

They banter a bit over potential alternatives, knowing that whatever happens and wherever the dust falls, it likely will be different than anything either of them suggest.

The principal holds out an assortment of papers in the direction of Aartemann's hand, which is already full of papers to carry home. The new stack forces the emptying of hands, and for the moment, departure is delayed. Immediately Gene mentions office staff will cover art classes for an opportunity for Aartemann to work on the papers. In puzzlement Aartemenn looks for a heading or a title while trying to identify what new committee or activity he now is assigned work for. With the county fine arts festival only three days away, and duty with the festival steering committee—which has consumed much of any extra time for the past two weeks—he has small patience for added tasks. His face unavoidably screams the worry and frustration silently felt. He's never been good at hiding frustration when it is past the end of the workday. Besides, this day has proved to be packed and stressful and his fatigue can only be relieved when he has reached home.

"I've nominated you for teacher of the year," Gene hastens to say apparently sensing the edge felt by Aartemann at the end of this day.

"No, I don't want it. Someone else! Really! Man oh man, now I'll have to go to the end of the year teacher breakfast. I was going to skip it and work here. Really!"

"Nobody wants it. You deserve it!" and he goes on making points in the teacher's favor, but all the time Aartemann is thinking of having to attend the breakfast which will cause his last day's work to be unfinished.

He has a doctor's appointment in the afternoon of that day to have both eyes retested. With the year end work undone, he would have to return to school on the first day of summer vacation to close up the art room. What should be taken as an honor is instead another time disaster for his brain to absorb, and at the most tiresome point of his day.

The principal jokes, "You can do like they do at the Oscars and have a taped acceptance speech on a large screen," and he demonstrates miming a thank you talk in front of a camera while swinging a golf club on some imagined tee at the local course.

The two men are a similar pair, each easily able to read the thoughts of the other. They are friends as well as being two of the few male members of the elementary staff. Both are always open and honest with each other. They have the same odd sense of humor that often tends to feed off the other, creating a banter they normally enjoy. At the moment, Aartemann is caught off guard, and although he smiles at the principal's pantomime, the fatigue he feels stops any humorous retaliation.

"There is no way I can get things ready for a sub while trying to get ready for the festival, teach classes, and prepare for the year end; and I was going to take next Wednesday off for an appointment, and I found out just yesterday that I have to help make and serve a retirement breakfast (since he is on that committee as well) at 7:45 A.M on that day so I'll have to come to school at least in the morning, but I have to take the afternoon off for the appointment and ... ," he silences his words and realizes he is rambling and Gene is staring.

His respect for Gene guides his thoughts and response now.

"I'll take it home and look through it and see what you need. Are you sure there is not someone else? I really appreciate it, the thought, but really I do not care for it."

"I've already sent in your name."

This feels to Aartemann more like a casket lid slamming for some reason.

"Of course you realize it is just our school's nomination, but I think you should win the corporation selection. You should be Teacher of the Year. You do so much for our students, with your art knowledge, caring, and humor."

"Man, what if I win, I'll have to walk to the front and accept the award at the breakfast."

His thoughts make it no more desirable but it seems inevitable that the nomination will stand. Perhaps it will look and feel better at home. He tosses the papers in the case for a later review. All he can read quickly is the top bold face line: Application Procedure. This sounds like a job not an award. Aartemann doesn't mention that fact to Gene.

"Good news, bad news."

She describes several facets of the phone conversation with a past Florida friend and the friend's new romantic discovery, which sounds very much like a story she and Aartemenn have lived through in their own life. His wife is excited for her old friend and beams for her. Listening and watching her animation over the events he consumes handfuls of nuts from a bag of deluxe mixed. He believes stress eating relaxes the tension carried home from the school day, especially the final fifteen minutes. His doctor would disagree.

"I've got good news and bad news too, Gail," he starts after a pause following her story completion.

Aartemann already sees a major conflict going on inside of him. A coveted award for some is turning rapidly into an albatross for the over-extended, over-stressed art teacher, and he can not for the life of him figure out exactly why. His wife will be proud, he thoughtfully acknowledges. Why is he not? His mind is running faster than his words.

After explaining the situation, she is proud, yet puzzled over his distress. As they talk on, with him checking out the six stapled pages the principal had handed to him, he realizes he is talking loudly. He is demonstratively, vocally, agitatedly, stressing out. Expressing his feelings of anger begins to calm him as nothing has yet.

Only mildly panicky now, Aartemann asks himself silently, *How do I pull myself together and out of this? Bigger question, what is this I need to dig out of? What is happening to me? What is wrong here? Why am I spazzed out over a title of teacher of the year?*

He grabs a paperback novel, *Cold Mountain*, and heads for the patio to try to relax and finish the final dozen pages he has left to read. This is where he left off, as he put himself to bed the night before. Reading is slow tonight, since his mind is on the pages of the application more than the novel ending. He sets the book aside, sits in the swing, listens to the birds, and lets his head spin in the opposite direction from the brain cyclones inside it. Emotions are in overdrive and with stress, on a collision course. That much is certain of. Why? He yet has no clue.

"Why?" Aartemann puzzles aloud now to himself and to the birds.

The couple eats their supper, mostly in silence, in the patio swing. Gail has made a wilted spinach dish from the new cookbook Aartemann brought home as a gift for her. The spinach is wilted with a dressing of hot Balsamic vinegar, a bit of sugar, and oil, with green onion tops and bacon bits added. Delicious! They talk about the delights of the food, and some other spring favorites—strawberries, asparagus, etc. They avoid talking about the award. But his mind and heart struggle with grief, anger, memories, frustration, stress, and a handful of other negatives that are being stirred mentally in with the offer of an award—an award meant to be positive. He decides over the spinach that he can not accept the award and thus will have to word process on the computer after supper. Can he make some words explain why? He hid the fact he was near tears over the thing. Why?

Click, click. Microsoft Word. Go! He sits, stares again at the six application pages, drinks coffee that his wife sets beside the keyboard, and again battles tears. *This is the darndest thing,* is his silent thought, or does he say it aloud? Gail is quiet, sitting on the sofa behind him, likely praying, for she knows he is troubled in some way. She does not know why.

The phone rings and a recognized two-year-old voice begins to talk on the answering machine typically in use to screen the calls. The receiver is snatched up quickly.

This is an important call. Gail beats him to the call, but very soon he gets his own extension, and all three are on together. The grandson jabbers away, answering questions using a speech form neither Gail nor he can decode but relish with such delight. Tears finally fall from his cheeks, but for a different reason. Aartemann's smiles are reflected in these tears. Some sanity seems to return. The call ends with satisfaction and delight and the task at the computer is faced again, with less stress and more determination to find words to put this thing in a somewhere else world. A world of behind, rather than of future.

Aartemann's return to the computer now finds words and his old typing skills, learned in a high school typing class owning only one electric typewriter, are paying off. He processes his heart and soon is running spell check. His spelling accuracy never equals his writing speed but this effort is better than average. Gail is reading still behind him, smiling as his progress shows, and is assured her prayers are being answered.

"Thank you, Lord," Gail whispers between sentences of her book which has momentarily fallen into her lap.

Aartemann prints three copies of the page and proof-reads from the first copy as the second and third are being inked.

> The application's six pages of information that included a required page count limit of 26 pages will be strictly followed in number but the Application Procedure Portfolio Guidelines gave no good directives for declining involvement. Thus, I shall attempt my own content style.

The guidelines specifically search for someone other than myself. I feel somewhat honored that anyone might at first consider me a contender for such an award, but I honestly know myself to be short of what is desired. The basic data I own is only that being a name, an address, and a score of years plus of paid instructional employment. The five plus years of education, culminating in a Life Teaching License are documented somewhere, in a box in the attic perhaps, but fail to record the real training which came in the first five years of classroom responsibility. How many dozen score of those trainings, classes, associations, committees, task groups, offices, and observations took place over two decades and went unrecorded and are now lost to memory? Most are unavailable to a now required outline.

A teacher of the year likely would have had a loftier reason for entering the profession than simple job security as a green college freshman, especially when that security was gone by the time the bachelor's degree was attained. But it is more in the living through the job, year after year, that the higher reasons for educating children become a part of a teacher's soul.

Greatest accomplishments, pathetic compared to those of a true mover and shaker, include receiving a gift of a pair of dried brown fall leaves from the playground, all that child of poverty could afford. Another child was heard saying in the grocery, "That's my art teacher!" He entered my class two years earlier able to speak only four words. An acknowledgement of a job done well is best from a student that comes bearing a home drawn picture using the skills taught just a week earlier in my class. Hearing, "Art is my favorite," from a child bests any teacher of the year plaque. These and the like are my art teacher accomplishments.

My current community involvement by guideline definition is zero. Ten years ago I would have struggled with the one typed, double-spaced page limit. The American way filled every moment with groups, clubs, and volunteering, civic and church activity. A forced new life taught the higher achievement of closer relationships, not greater involvement. Priorities changed to: God, wife, God, family, God, wife, myself, God, and a few occasional activities when God points the direction. It's not an award-winning list, but the few lucky enough to follow it need fewer counselors and capsules. Some tag it as introverted, negatively. My Lord stamps it with extraordinary peace, love, and joy.

As for philosophy, issues, trends, and the profession-that's best left to the politicians. They have answers. No need trying to write words they want to hear when they already have the wheel. Accountability is really their belief in me. Officials wanting to prove me of some worth look for a scale. I rate accountability with student smiles in a classroom. I add to that, every moment a child sees, hears, touches, smells, or can say something new, something unknown a second earlier. Multiply the sum by their joy level. Learning can be exciting and desirable. Bonus points are given for child initiated hugs and multiplied if the child gets none at home. Tally the score and you have an accountability scale that reaches kids, saves playgrounds full of children, but gets no election votes, no Nobel prizes, and no framed certificates.

You look for a Teacher of the Year for the school who can compete for state Teacher of the Year. I'm not that teacher!

So you see, my lists are weak, and not of the desirable nature. I beg permission to decline a nomination for teacher of the year. Perhaps another time I will be known not as "the teacher" but as "the taught." My education rank is a master teacher, but my reality is having been taught by The Master, saved by grace.

"Done. Job complete. Over."

Trying to get into a new book's story goes nowhere, since the three-hour plus ordeal of writing the refusal left a head ache behind both eyes and his temples throbbing. She rubs without words being spoken to soothe the pain. The pain is as inward as outward. As mental as physical. She suggests and he consents to bedtime. She rubs his back while he lays facing away from her. It put them both to sleep. Aartemann awakes in turmoil. He sleeps again. He wakes. He thinks. He sleeps. He wakes. He frets. He sleeps only to awake and sleep and awake and sleep over and over and over all through the night.

Breakfast is largely silent, with stares out the window.

Thoughts are still trying to make sense of the event and the emotions. Gail and he talk of cats and kittens and of a new brown and white one who came for its first visit to their patio.

Gene is not in the principal's office when Aartemann arrives. He soon returns after dropping off an armload in the art room and finds his school leader. Handing off the response, Aartemann fights tears. He tries to explain why he can not in any way accept the nomination. Gene is thanked for the offer, accepted as a compliment, and Aartemann can not really explain what has happened to him, except it has taken him back to a time of grief over his past life. For some unknown reason, the potential award serves as a trigger. Gene really seems to understand, like all things in life that the two discuss honestly together. He accepts the letter, word processed the night before. He drops it to his desk to be read later, presumably.

Finally it is done. Finally the mental pain is leaving.

Will I still have to attend the breakfast?

It is a mental question Aartemann is afraid to ask. In the final week of school his conscience will answer. *Yes!*

The now more relaxed art teacher sits down to a fresh cup of coffee from the thermos and brings up eBay on his computer. Hitting the buttons like a pro, he finds the pair of auctions on which he has bids placed and finds he is still in the lead with no other bidders. It seems, other than Aartemann, very few eBay buyers have the desire for the old Irish, Scottish and British novels from the turn of the century. He gets a bit embarrassed going home so often and confessing he has bought another old book. He often buys to add to the full bookshelf of his to-be-read-later collection. He does get off easy with Gail since he seldom pays more for the book than the shipping costs. She calls it his "retirement library." She is generous with him in many ways. He is financially tighter in spending than he is poor. Mostly, he just gets a kick out of finding a fun old book at the bargain-basement price.

Next he types in the web site for the on line edition of USA *Today* and clicks go. It is a routine he goes through almost every day, if there is a five minute break in the morning—check eBay bids and read the headlines in USA *Today*. He seldom reads a story and if he does it is likely only a single paragraph or sentence. He checks the Dow, even though he has no stock. He has a small retirement mutual fund but he always says that if he needs that for retirement, the amount is so small he will likely be pushing a wheeled walker down the school hallway before he can afford to retire. Right now it would not be enough to fund last Christmas' school staff holiday party.

The headlines are like most have been for the past many weeks. It's coming up on a presidential election year and everything is election news. He spots a small story about the Indiana primary about to take place. Indiana is never a hotbed for national politics in a presidential election. Indiana electoral college votes have about as much chance of going anything other than Republican as finding Elvis' bones in Johnny Appleseed's Fort Wayne grave site. And by the time Indiana gets around to having their primary election, the candidates have already been selected by the voting in all of the other states prior to Indiana's May affair. Aartemann grumbles to himself at the attempt at the political hype and then gets an idea. He is sometimes dangerous with an idea.

Aartemann zips to his email and types in All Staff. For a heading he writes "the ultimate solution.." Then he types in his new brain burst.

> I just got a terrific idea for the solution to needed presidential election reform, at least for the Indiana primary. Forget all primaries throughout the country. Henceforth all elections will take place on November 2nd. The President will travel to his home state and go to the polling location and enter the voting booth to cast his vote. When he exits from behind the curtain, if he sees his shadow, he will get four more years. This message is not intended to represent any political persuasion, nor is it paid for by any candidate or political party.

Aartemann clicks on the send button and smiles. He can't wait for the replies to begin to come back from those staff on the receiving end of his cyberthought.

Aartemann's first class enters the art room just after he finishes the dregs from the bottom of his coffee mug. He bites the grounds that were allowed to pass by a collapsed coffee maker filter. Even Starbucks dregs are good. The thought of the soggy bean grounds cause his smile.

The fifth graders seem eager as they begin finding seats assigned months ago and never changed during the year. Aartemann grabs their projects folder and watches the final half of the class enter while standing at attention, silently, smilingly, in the front of the room.

"Ronald'll be late. He's got 'is head stuck in uh chair," a student announces with a face full of glee.

Aartemann's eyes roll to the top of his head, he cocks his head to his right, his arms drop straight to his sides but still hang on to the folder of pictures, and his mouth slowly opens … wordless. A few snickers are heard as the last of the class sits down.

Aartemann stands silently for over a full minute. A minute of silence is equal to hours of torture for an elementary student. Around the room in at least three locations, different students or pairs of students are desperately trying to contain their laughter.

Aartemann looks down at himself, then to the class and asks, "Did I do something?"

Kent, one of the snickering boys replies, "No, Ronald is late 'cause he got his head stuck in a chair."

With the disclosure, he can hold back no longer and erupts in laughter and so follows the remainder of the class.

Aartemann smiles and says nothing but thinks to himself, *Ah, I'm teacher of the year now, the right way. Back to normal, what a treat. Life is true again.*

He begins giving the art directions for the completion of the project and before he is finished, red-eared Ronald stealths his way in to his seat, obviously embarrassed. In pity for him, Aartemann instructs on and draws no additional attention to the lad.

Administrative Professional Assistants' Day

Mr. Aartemann is busy in the pre-student arrival time of this morning. Student-free time is normally referred to as teacher preparation time, but it is often a period filled with everything administration is hired to produce to eliminate these paid preparation hours. Or so it seems! It is a regular morning, filled with much computer activity answering emails. The bulk of correspondence has to do with an upcoming arts festival. Others are over illness reports of a former colleague and friend, and informational notices sent out from the office as well as other staff. For jollification, a couple of really good e-jokes arrive that have been forwarded and forwarded till it takes longer to open a window with the message than it does to read the script. He sends himself emails to his home computer to replace memory notes in the shirt pocket, a habit long ago developed. The pocket note memory technique was prior to his limited technology education. Now he emails himself, knowing his memory may forget where he lays the sticky notes. E-mail is efficient and almost foolproof. E-mail is Aartemann's friend. So now he emails; Aartemann to Aartemann. He is mid-sentence of that email as the announcement is cast from the not so techy old-fashioned wood speaker above the chalkboard.

"Would all staff please very quickly go to the teacher's lounge? Everyone come as quickly as possible."

The announcement is in a softer voice than the normal. Different from the voice accustomed to making announcements, with a sure direct approach. But it is recognizable as one of the third grade teaching staff.

He has to finish his sentence and send the e-mail message. It is a delaying activity because he established long ago, on outgoing email, an automatic spellchecker task. It is necessary as a result of his limited proficiency in that spelling area. Always it seems a disgrace to Aartemann when he receives an email from another educator with spelling errors, missing capitalization or punctuation, or other things that should not be left without a bright crimson ink checkmark. Many teachers overlook in their own e-mails the errors they would chastise their students for not correcting. It happens in business too, he is told. It is an ugly side to technology.

With the e-mail on its way, he makes his way toward the lounge not really so far from his door.

It is often a bad omen to get such an announcement, last minute, no explanation, just urgency. It so often relates to a staff person's sudden illness, a death, or some other tragic event that needs immediate explanation face to face eliminating unnecessary false rumor variations. What could this one be? We'll know soon, he speaks inwardly to himself as he notices no other staff is yet in the hallway of the lounge. With voices being heard in a mumble around the corner, all seem to be moving immediately toward the lounge. He takes the time to return to his own room and pull supplies from the shelves and places them on tables for the first arriving class. He wants to be as ready as possible since he doesn't know what the meeting is about or how long it might last. He returns to the hall and now is likely the last to arrive. On and on his memory of other hastily called stand-up meetings race through recall. Most being negative in nature, he prepares for the worst.

He stops and plants himself in a corner behind the entire staff that is now waiting in the hall outside the lounge door.

The third grade teacher, June Long, the same that had made the announcement plea, begins, "I heard last night, Cindy heard it too, on the radio that today is Administrative Assistants' Day. We thought it was Friday and planned on doing a traditional thing on Friday. So we didn't even have time to call the rest of the committee. We hurriedly put together what we could and decided we would celebrate Secretaries' Day, or Administrative Assistants' Day, or whatever it's called, for the rest of the week. We were so afraid we were wrong and we are sorry we could not call everyone, and I hurried and made a pan of caramel pecan rolls and they are in the lounge for breakfast this morning and there is some fruit juice to go along with it, and we have something for Jill and, and I even called Hallmark to find out what day was correct since one of my calendars gave Wednesday and one was Thursday and the lesson planner calendar says Wednesday, today, and we thought it was Friday, and it has always been on a Friday, and Hallmark said it was Friday."

And then she finally takes a breath.

Many seem to breathe deeper now that the reason for the meeting is revealed. It is not a disaster of great magnitude at all. It is a relief obvious on the faces of several, since the last stand-up meeting announced the departure of a custodian due to the diagnosis of cancer and the need to be closer to a special hospital for treatment with the prognosis not looking well at all. Another stand-up meeting of the year dealt with another staff person's spouse and a sudden unexpected death due to an accident. Odds are against good news when a stand-up meeting is called. June provides welcome news in her flustered, rapidly presented speech. Anguished faces slowly begin to grin throughout the hallway crowd.

Jill has been the school office secretary for some time now. She replaced another quite capable but different individual in a time when the job classification did not yet require a socially-correct title. It was a time when the title of school secretary was, for the most part, an honorable title. Who changed it?

James, the prior secretary, had done a fantastic job for a dozen years and left in good standing. Of course, James was not her real name any more than Administrative Professional Assistant to the Administrative Principal was her real title. James was just the secretary. Aartemann called her James because he'd seen so many others treat her like a butler or slave. He always apologized to James when he requested her to do something for himself. Unfortunately there were a few; there always is a few, who thought she was also their own personal secretary. They would leave papers to be duplicated with notes on the exact number and what was to be stapled together and which needed to be hole punched and what color each page should be printed on, and exactly what time they would be returning for the materials—or could she deliver? They are likely the reason for the socially acceptable change of the title.

James was a good-looking blonde with a shape to match the hair and fair face. James was, however, not a dumb blonde by any means. James was loyal, happy, energetic, and as fast as lightning in responding to any request, regardless of who made the request. James was sometimes a bit flirty. Suggestive jokes occasionally spilled from her mouth. She spoke openly about home activities that could bring blushes to some of the men. They were the only part of the staff that the "flirty" had effect on. Since the school is a typical elementary, James had few males to practice her ornery jokes and comments upon. James was the kind of gal that could get away with it because everyone knew, however enticing she could sound; it was not a true reflection of her actions and behavior. Even many of the ladies got a kick out of seeing her in action, bringing men to silence and color.

James held the look and quality wished for by every male professional who has ever needed a secretary. James looked the type described in novels that spent a large portion of the day on her employers' lap. But in reality, this school's James was nothing close to the image she portrayed, and everyone knew it. It is part of what made her so much fun, part of what made her James. Jill replaced James and is probably even more able to do the job, just as much fun and also ornery, but in different ways.

When James resigned to move on to another post with higher pay, it was announced in a stand-up staff meeting. There was open weeping. Not just by the men.

———————

"It's supposed to be Friday," comments Jill (Jill Schwartenbarger, but no one ever tries to pronounce her last name, or write it) as she exits a storage room beside the lounge to join the assembled group in the hall. Jill obviously has overheard at least a portion of the explanation coming from June about her Hallmark inquiry.

June disappears into the lounge as Jill appears. She quickly reappears with something large wrapped in colored tissue and dangling an enveloped card between two of her fingers. She presents the gift to Jill and again explains that we will be honoring Jill for all she does for us and celebrating all the rest of the week.

"That should cover all of the calendars," June explains as Jill lifts off the tissue and holds up a large potted plant with cascading flowers on vines.

Cindy, having sneaked by the proceedings and entered the lounge, emerges with her own announcement.

"We also will have Dairy Queen ice cream cake in the freezer for you to have at noon time or whenever you desire. Don't forget where it is and don't forget to eat some. I hurried out last night after June and I talked on the phone to pick up a cake. You know how you can always go into Dairy Queen and pick up a pre-made cake. I've never had any trouble before having many to choose from. Well, last night there was a very small selection. Figures! So, (pause) Jill's cake has the Superman shield decoration on its top."

She tipped the cake in the direction of the majority of the staff.

"I wanted to have Jill's name put on it but the workers were high school students and you know how they spell. When I took the cake to the counter I was pleased to see the owner also acting as the evening manager. At the register he reached to take the money and he asked if I wanted anything written on the cake. Of course then, I said yes. I asked him to put Jill Superwoman on the cake to make it look like something that related to Secretaries' Day. The only problem …" (pause) " … he spelled it with a second e. It says Jill Superwomen not Superwoman. So it is now presented as representing the entire gambit of different roles that Jill performs for all of us. She fills so many jobs that she is Superwomen."

Laughter grows from the group.

Cindy continues once quiet is somewhat restored, "And we have another cake if this one is not enough. We have this sailboat ice cream cake also." She concludes amid more laughing and joking as Cindy displays high over her head the second cake, hastily retrieved from the lounge.

"Don't drop it!" someone shouts.

Mr. Aartemann talks a bit with some of the other staff and eventually heads for his door-duty, since the students will be entering the building very soon. He intentionally avoids the caramel pecan rolls, locally famous when made by June. Pounds are not yet eliminated from his last vacation's weight gain.

Tornados are the talk of several students as they enter the building from the busses that delivered them. The previous night had been stormy and several sightings had been made. Some were official. Sirens had sounded in warning multiple times in town.

"I saw two of them."

"One came right over our house. I saw the eye of the tornado."

"It t-t-touched down right b-behind our h-house, b-but, b-b-but, but it didn't h-hurt anything."

"We saw it."

"I went outside to play with Beth next door and the tornado came so I ran home and went in the basement. Did you go to the basement?"

"The tornado blew our trash can over."

"Are we going to have tornados tonight again?"

"I don't know, only God knows that, but probably not tonight," Mr. Aartemann calmly encourages, trying to relieve the mild panic still in the young girl's eyes.

Once the last student files down the hall toward their home room he returns to the lounge and eats half of a pecan roll. Later, a wedge of ice cream cake becomes his very own. Alone, he enjoys the wedge of ice cream as much as if it had been a Black Angus tenderloin steak. He loves Dairy Queen ice cream cake, diet or no diet.

Tossing his paper plate away in the trash and the spoon in the "dirties tray" as it is called, Aartemann turns to leave and Abs enters.

"Where were you this morning, Abs? There are gooey rolls here and DQ cakes in the freezer to celebrate secretaries' something or other. You missed the presentation but I saved some of the cake just for you. I could have eaten it all. You missed the door duty again. That's nothing new—do you remember you've had door duty all this year, like last year? You remember the school door? Okay, what's the grin? My fly open?"

"I'm leaving."

"Oh, want me to cut you a piece of cake first? It's good."

"No, I mean I'm leaving the school. At the end of the year."

"Oh!"

"Is that all, just oh?"

"Well it's a surprise. I'm the one that was considering retirement. You're too young. Your still smiling, what's up?"

"He asked me to marry him."

"Who?"

"Who do you think?"

"Paul?"

She nods.

"Paul Williams?"

"Yes, of course."

"What'd ya say?"

"You curmudgeon."

"Yes, huh?"

"Yes-s-s."

"Boy, this place is falling apart fast. I better get out myself. Hey, I'm really happy for you. You deserve it, really. I mean that," and he gives her a big hug that no staff sees. "Told anyone else?"

"Not yet, I'll talk to Gene as soon as I can this morning."

"There'll be no grass growing between your exit and mine. I think I've made up my mind. I'll stop by at noon. I want details. I'll fill you in on my own and show you my letter. It's typed and printed, just not sent yet. Rumor is the redistricting is going to happen and this place will be shut down. Most of these students will go to the new building to be opened next year. Not much reduction in staff but relocation for all, most to the new place, likely—my guess, no announcement yet. I don't think I can start over. I've been packing for weeks now in anticipation of a move or retirement. I think retirement is the way. What will I do at school without you to pester anyhow? I'll see you at noon, and I have a prep period right after so I want all of the fine details. All of it ... well, not the sweet stuff, of course. Make us a fresh pot of coffee in your little thingy. Oops, I've got a class, gotta run. Bye."

Aartemann stops at the door and looks back.

"I really am happy for you, Abs. Can you do sweet?" and he is gone.

The Festival

This particular day of school seems to be running at mach speed, with stressors carrying payloads of annoying interferences to tasks and the schedule. Routine is seemingly a word as extinct around here as the dinosaurs. Even the morning starts with another preschool stand-up staff meeting in the hall outside the office on the opposite side of the state … the state of confusion. The information released is the intent of the corporation's superintendent to recommend the school board to approve and proceed with one particular redistricting plan. A recommendation of the closing of this school will be included. The rumor has been circulating for a month and more. Like the threat of a hurricane, everyone knew it would hit, just not when.

"All jobs are secure, but everyone will necessarily be reassigned if the school board agrees to the proposal, which is expected," Gene announces.

This just confirms what all of the staff has already resigned themselves to. It means more moving boxes will be needed soon. These, like most teachers' resources, will necessarily be provided by the individual staff members. It's like a factory closing. Jobs are offered at another location but the moving task is left to the employee. Moving cost was not in the teacher contract, nor is it in the new building construction budget. It's in no budget.

It's not my problem, if I retire, Aartemann thinks. It is another sign confirming his retirement plans.

Principal Gene also announces on a more positive note, that our school counselor, Abby Sledford, has accepted a proposal of marriage, but will be completing the year with us. Again, no comments and hardly any surprise since the rumor mill always at work in the school had already alerted the entire staff before school ended yesterday. Only the principal is left out of the rumor loop. He fails to understand the lack of response. There is a delayed applause, a few hand shakes and pats on the back for Abs. Aartemann just rolls his eyes noting in his mind the wasted time the two announcements took from his needed preparations for the rest of the day. He quickly returns to tasks in the art room.

The school day happens.

It is over three hours after the normal teacher work day when he arrives at his house and has a chance to slow down from the hectic pace that goes along with serving on the steering committee for, and participating in, an arts festival. He had two schools' art displays to set up since he was helping another teacher struggling with a medical problem. Time is also consumed by an area he is responsible for where art projects will be made at the festival site. He had, in a weak moment, consented to head up this year's festival hands-on activities. Just this morning he finally finished entering, in calligraphy, the individual names of students participating in the festival onto achievement certificates. Other fine arts teachers just use a ballpoint and long hand them on. Why can he not be like them? Why is he such a perfectionist in some things? But now the day is festively complete and things that he is responsible for are now in place. All he needs to do is some waiting. *Get some rest*, is his main thought, *and get up early to get to the site of the festival prior to the thousands of visitors. It will be another long day tomorrow.*

———————

Within ten minutes of arriving home the phone rings and the every-other-word conversation able to be heard from the caller suggests correctly that the call is being made from a cell. And while the caller is driving.

"We're a' … 'he Rockvi' exit ri.' .t now," comes the reply to "Where are you?" The Rockville exit has to refer to the county's stone road leading to the blister of a town of forty-seven inhabitants that is just a mile and a quarter north of the highway coming toward Aartemann's home. That will put them only about ten minutes away. They are not expected for another hour. That estimate is made by both Aartemann and Gail, based on how long it could take for their son to get off work, he and his wife to pre-pare themselves and their two small boys for travel, then begin their trek northward, probably stopping for a fast-food supper along the way.

"Did you eat?"

Since Pa Aartemann has not yet done so, is too tired to care, although his wife does have a sauce pot of hominy heating on the range, he has to assume the earlier arrival is due to omitting a food stop delay.

"Ye,' we go' fas' 'ood when we left 'ome, but I'm real' 'oking 'ward to a B&K breaded cheeseburger an' … roo' beer. Did you eat?"

"No, I just got home ten minutes ago. You are really breaking up. I can only hear about half of what you say. I got the B&K root beer and a breaded cheeseburger part. Okay. Got some hominy here ready, but a Coney dog does sound good. When you get here, we'll go out and get something. Bring the kids here first. See you in a couple minutes."

"Okay, we're pas' th' Smith 'ouse if 'ey stil' … click … buzz."

What a delightful evening everyone seems to have including the two-year-old and eight-month-old grandsons who love it when a train passes on the tracks just to the west of the Aartemann property.

"Can I ride on that train?" the oldest grandson repeatedly asks his mom or dad, every time another train's whistle blows.

Another long freight train passes. The trains are as magical an experience for him, and his younger by fourteen months brother, as Disney World, the Eiffel Tower, or skydiving is for adults. After all, he has spent the "grown up" half of his life enthralled with *Thomas the Train* in everything from pj's and DVD's to wooden toys. Thomas has come to life before his very eyes.

"Train!" he repeats. "Can I ride?"

It's all a part of the excitement of this first visit since five months ago. Almost a year—eleven months—has passed since they all slept overnight. What fun the evening is with all new toys for the gran's. New words are heard from the gran's by the grandparents, and the boys' mom and dad are getting something of a break from having to provide all the attention to the boys. The night goes so fast that the older two year and eight-month-old brother are still going strong well past bedtime. A couple of hours past bedtime, in fact. Pa Aartemann, just plain Pa to the small boys, tries to calm him for bed by reading a book to him inside a backpacker's tent he had set up in the corner of the living room. That works for three pages, less than three minutes. Several other failed attempts are followed by a trip upstairs to the antique full size bed which the boy has decided earlier in the evening to be "mine" bed. He lies down with little fuss, sings "Jesus Loves Me" in a whisper, so as not to awaken his brother in the next room. With the accompanying voices of his mom and grandpa, the song ends and now he is saying his prayers with mom. Mr. Aartemann exits quietly to the downstairs, to a cup of fresh coffee, and the first opportunity to rest his educationally swollen feet.

"Mom?" Overhead the wee voice, but a husky voice uncommon from a two and a half year old, floats down from the upper bedroom. Silence from all adults downstairs is an attempt to encourage the child's sleep, instead of additional conversation.

"Mom!" resounds from above a bit louder four minutes later.

Silence.

A train passes in the darkness of the night. All adults hope that it will not wake sleeping children. It is a busy track, and Friday night is the busiest night as freights head home for the weekend. Saturday is the slowest shipping day normally. Sunday makes up for the Saturday traffic lull.

"Can I ride that train?"

Faces turn red with the stifle of laughs from grand-parents and redder from frustration on a young mother of a "terrible two." The two-year-old wannabe engineer's dad is already fast asleep in a wide soft chair, belly down, with stockinged feet hanging over the ottoman. A short quiet interval holds as the train's noise evaporates to the southern horizon.

"Hell-oo-o?"

It is astonishing and uncontrollably comical hearing the young boy use three syllables for the hello word. The questioning end inflection is just like a current trendy expression well beyond what a two-year-old should understand. Stifling grandparent giggles, they are wise not to ask where the young lad heard that word used in just that way. And his now exasperated mother is redder than before and moving on her way toward the stairs. A new plan is being formed as she is underway to the yet wide awake two-year-old. And with that Godly mother, there is no doubt; prayers are being said by her even as she makes the stairs.

Mr. Aartemann has an early arising, after the short sleep of the night. Silence shares a time alone resting in a swing on his patio with a hot cup of Starbucks coffee he brewed himself by pushing a single button. The real work in creating the cup of coffee came the night prior by his wife. Gail filled the basket filter with the fresh ground beans, measured the right amount of water and had not only the coffee maker in place, ready for the sunrise, but also a mug for the old art teacher to use. Since he awakes prior to the alarm and turns it off, he is able to get out of bed without waking her. Thus he pushes the brew button alone. Now he swings the swing, kicks up his heels, and drinks a dark stiff heavy brew created by sneaking a cup before even half of the pot of water has flowed through the beans. It is a thick European style coffee delight. This cup is as strong as a Starbucks coffee shop purchase, but the location is better—pond side.

Eventually sleepers in all beds awake. Shortly Mrs. Aartemann prepares a breakfast. Some partake while Mr. Aartemann holds a grandson in the lap the swing makes of his legs. Pa teaches the boy that red is a cardinal, yellow is a finch; the noisiest sound comes from a crow. A fish is the splash in the water at the end of the bridge—which is the word the grandson uses for the wooden pier. A train passes with over sixty hopper cars labeled Herzog, so the swinging pair decide the train's name is Herzog and it is probably going down the track to visit Thomas the Train. He doesn't ask Pa if he can ride that train. He likes his seat. Both do.

Mr. Aartemann has a very hard time leaving home in time to get to the fine arts festival. Duty, however, calls. He arrives in plenty of time and is the day's first concession purchaser.

"Is the coffee good coffee? I'll have a cup. How much is it? No sugar or cream, just black. Nope, no donut, I'm fat enough. Just the coffee, thanks. Mmm, it's good! I'll be back." And steering committee member Aartemann heads off to make sure the first art activity is established and ready to go. It will be clay modeling presented by an art teacher from a local parochial school. He has time then to get a second cup of coffee and experience the first musical presentation that follows a short theatrical production. Perhaps soon he will look at a few of the hundreds or thousands of art projects on display before he makes his own art activity presentation scheduled after the clay session.

His time, his turn arrives. He puts on the black top hat with the Mickey Mouse plastic ears extended out the sides that was purchased at Disney World and actually used in his wedding. It was worn at the reception time just for the cake cutting. His grandson had helped him string fluorescent beads on a hat band the night before and they attract much attention. Mr. Aartemann announces to anyone entering the festival's main entrance that he is Beadman—ready and willing to teach anyone, regardless of age, the skills needed to make a bracelet. It takes a bit of coaxing to get the first recruit but that young boy walks to the tabled work area followed by two slightly older sisters and a mom who is slightly shamed into participating. Each chooses a favorite color of chenille wire for their work from the bundle held by Beadman's waist belt.

"Step one!" he announces loud enough to attract the attention of anyone within a baseball's throw of his top hat. "Bend the wire's end over one finger. Step one, one finger."

They do it.

"Step three!" is the shout. "Twist the hooked end three times into a loop. Step three, three twists."

Beadman congratulates each participant of the family of four as they accomplish the wire look of a mini lasso.

The young boy, recognizing the wire is now ready to string beads since the directions are also on a picture step-by-step poster lying on the worktable, asks, "What happened to step two?"

"Oh, yea, glad you reminded me," Beadman responds, acting forgetful in a terribly overly dramatic fashion, like the worst actor in a community theater production. "This is step two ..." and he cups his hands about his mouth, looks at the ceiling and hoots like an owl.

"Who-ho, who-ho!"

It is done quite loudly, again attracting attention from many passing by who are now wondering what the art activity is that is creating such a fuss and sounding like a nature trail sortie. Conversations at the information booth between other steering committee members come to an immediate halt, due to the screeching who-ho's. Amazingly the boy immediately sounds the call, as instructed. Then he begins beading his wire with his own desired assortment of neon colored beads. The two girls look at each other and do not so vigorously follow his call. The mother muffles her call by bending her head into her left arm pit and the family all begin enjoying bead selection together. Participation is proving once and for all that the family that who-ho's together also enjoys beading together.

Another pair of young children join the event by the time the owl calls are complete and Beadman begins sharing the directions again, just as loud, since the vocal activity is attracting attention and takers to the art activity. When the missing second step is discovered and the question asked and the hooting sound step demonstrated, Beadman turns to the quad family and invites them to once again join in the second step if they would choose. He makes it quite clear it is not mandatory. The boy participates.

And so it goes for ten minutes longer than what is scheduled for the art activity session. Beadman has gotten the job as a result of another artist and former art teacher having to cancel his anticipated activity of doing Native American Indian beadwork. That teaching was also to include training in the colors preferred by the Native Americans. So Beadman is a last minute replacement who is proving to be a very simple, fun, and successful replacement. The children of all ages, several parents of similar mixed ages, and a couple of probable grandparents (although Beadman is wise not to ask for ages) enjoy their beading art, almost as much as Beadman enjoys trying to embarrass himself.

A couple of hours later returns one of the families that beaded. Membership includes a mom with child on hip, her daughter of about grade three, and a son perhaps preschool or kindergarten. They stop to watch a final session of Model Magic sculpturing during which the walking age boy wants to participate, even though he has been involved in the first session of that activity. He could repeat in the second session if his mother will allow it. She is talking to one of the presenters and intends to leave soon. The boy lies down and kicks the tile floor as she ignores. The older sis can not get him up. She hides behind a post obviously embarrassed. Mortified! When mom finishes talking, the boy is now quiet but still prone and just as stubborn. Beadman, now back to his real role as Mr. Aartemann, steering committee member manning the information table, answers a question as to an upcoming performance desiring not to be missed by a patron. He catches the earlier mentioned family exiting out the main entrance doors. Mom, yet with babe on her left hip, pulls holding her right hand to the defiant disappointed boy's left. The sister's left hand is holding the right hand of her brother being literally drug from the festival. The moplike youth is not screaming, but legs are as useless as the proverbial wet dishrag. He is drug over the threshold of the double doors and is whisked, limp legged, behind the pulling ladies as the group disappears down the sidewalk. The doors' closers do the scene's curtain close. There goes a boy who did not want a good thing to end.

It is not a long time later that Mr. Aartemann has another occasion to be outside. Enjoyably he is putting away into his truck several items no longer needed for the day, and upon approaching the doors to reenter into the main foyer, he notices a mother and a small girl trailing behind her as they exit the "in" door. Mom holds the door for the little girl because both of her hands are busy holding opposite ends of a purple paper bird obviously created moments ago in the origami art project area. She holds it like it is Waterford Crystal, and to her it is just as valuable.

"I had fun!" is all he hears of her statement to mom.

Even art teachers, music teachers and committee members tire of talking only of the festival. Towards afternoon the conversations eventually get on to events of the area. Discussion gets to family events and items that need updating since some of the people involved get no other time for personal conversation other than this annual afternoon of the county arts festival. So tales of children and grands are shared. Pictures appear of course, and plans for the summer only a bit more than three week away are bragged about or simply vocally longed for. A change in next year's schedule in the area schools is an annual topic, for if no changes are eminent, there seems always the threat of it. And then pops up the topic of asparagus!

"I found this wonderful farm where they have several acres of asparagus and you can pick your own. It's $1.00 per pound. It is so good, so fresh. I like it raw."

"Ooo, not raw, but I do like it nuked just a bit till it is bright green but yet crisp and top it with just a bit of salt."

Mr. Aartemann has his own opinion of perfection when it comes to asparagus, a personal green favorite.

"It's a bit hard on us seniors. It is a natural diuretic, did you know? When you get to my age you don't need any more help in that area."

"I like it cooked soft, well done, with butter or crème sauce on top" is the opinion of a middle school art teacher who stops a spell and joins in on the vegetable conversation.

"Where is this place?" queries Aartemann as he grabs once again his four page printed program.

Notes written to himself surround the borders of half the pages. He copies the information for route twenty-two out of town toward a small country church, that he can remember being on a curve close to the golf course. Already forgetting the church name or denomination, he just writes "church," misspells that word, and from there the direction was to be a left.

"East?" he asks.

The steering committee director, who has already picked in the asparagus patch, turns herself to point south. She lifts and looks at her left arm, and answers.

"Yes, I guess that would be east."

She giggles at her need for time to think it through.

It takes a Midwesterner of the good ol' USA to give and take direction using north, south, east, and west. In so many places it has to be a right or a left, a fork, or follow a creek or some other landmark because to get from one point to another might require beginning the journey in the opposite direction because of curvy and winding roads. Some people just simply cannot get a head sense for map directions. Northwest could be simply any one of three hundred and sixty degree variables.

"It's about a mile or a bit after you turn at the church. There is an old house that is falling down, an old farmhouse, on the right just before you get to the lane. It's on the left."

She doesn't say north

Aartemann is much too busy writing while trying to get out of her the name. A spoken name comes out in three different forms all starting with "Wint something-or-other." Aartemann just scribbles down that beginning with what he thinks the first ending was. He's much too interested in an accurate account of the driving directions to look up and remind him of her hair color. He thinks about mentioning it, but decides against it, since he has a great deal of respect for the lady. This gal's a fun lady to be around, a former elementary art teacher, and a former teacher of the year. No, she is cool, and now he has access to fresh asparagus at one dollar a pound. Aartemann forgives her "blonde" directions.

"They had to mow all of it down last week after the frost but thought it should be ready to pick again this weekend."

She shares that information as well as a good bit of the conversation she had with the farm couple. The story explains how they had gotten the plants and prepared the land, all much more information than Aartemann is interested in. All he can see is inexpensive piles of asparagus fresher than any he has ever eaten. It will be as good as picking a tomato grown in a flowerbed (from his personal home Roma planting location) and eating it immediately after a wash (pronounced "worsh" locally) under the hose.

Getting hyper over pick-your-own asparagus is an

obvious senior trait oozing from an old art teacher who thinks most days more of retirement than Impressionism. Retirement and senioritis are beginning to show on him. Next may appear a fluorescent orange foam ball on the top of his Ford pickup's antenna, much to the embarrassment of his wife, Gail.

The day ends at the festival with ninety minutes of cleanup. Associated with packing up is a feeling of weakness and fever. He opts to stop downtown to retrieve a festival advertising banner he had hung the day after spring break, and finally a drive toward home. Of course he uses route twenty-two.

He sits in the swing, sharing all of the events of the festival, and munching with Gail the freshest asparagus they have ever eaten. Gail shares a couple of missed moments related to the morning hours of the grandboys' visit. The platter of asparagus is between them. Each spear is crispy. Each bite's taken just after a dip into a sprinkle of salt.

Salt of the earth.

Courtyard Drawing Safari

Aartemann makes it to school but ready for retirement. Having mailed a letter indicating interest, but not totally committing himself, he's mentally committed. The school is going to make changes. He sees an opportunity for a year or two of only working half a year. He could survive one semester each year, employed in an elementary building of the corporation which does not have full time art classes. It would be an ideal step. He asks about the situation in his letter and suggests he'd be interested. Aartemann already knows when the proposals go into place; he will be given first opportunity to choose his teaching location. Seniority over all the other art teachers is his possession. Some days he feels so old, he is certain he has seniority over Noah's sons. Today he is thinking more about days off during the upcoming summer and potential retirement than he is about the last few days of this school year.

It is such a great weather day outside. It is one of those days when any art teacher like Mr. Aartemann thinks of outdoor art. He so enjoys the out of doors himself. He sometimes wonders why he did not study to be a physical education teacher rather than the visual arts. He could have had a reason each day to go outside with every class. He is seen quite often looking at the gym teacher admiringly.

"My name's not Jim," she always says when she is

referred to as the gym teacher rather than the physical education instructor.

She is a bit testy when it comes to being called the gym teacher—rightly so.

Mr. Aartemann teases her plenty, telling her often that she should chill because, "I never mind being call Mr. Art Man."

Aartemann smiles.

He does not admire the gym teacher for her muscles and build even though most of the other (few) male elementary staff does. He drools over her tan. She tans well, and he does not. He figures if he had become a gym teacher he would be muscled, in shape, at least a shape other than a pear, and brown most of the year. He really, most of all, wanted to be a Beach Boy and surf the California beaches with babes screaming after him, but he can't swim, he can't sing, he can't tan, and he looks ridiculous with Bermuda shorts, a palm tree print shirt, and one of his goofy ties.

He has tried doing outside art class and usually it ends in disaster, with the paper and drawing materials blowing about. Images usually are incomplete and unlike nature. It is also extremely hard to keep a class of two dozen small tykes in tow and concentrating on drawing, when they are used to running and playing if they get a chance to set foot out of the school to the outdoors.

"P.E. teachers have it made," Aartemann has exclaimed more than once, or a hundred, perhaps a thousand times.

"The courtyard!"

Aartemann gets the great idea (remember, these are dangerous) of taking the first-grade class to the courtyard for their art lesson. It is unroofed, completely surrounded with walls, making it like a classroom—or a giant playpen, or a corral, or a jail cell, depending on how the primary students react. He hurriedly puts together a supply of paper, a stack of drawing boards made from old art room text covers that he cut off the aged books a couple generations ago after a new book adoption, and a large brown plastic tray of broken crayons that should be enough to supply even the wildest color chooser for the entire outdoor period. Besides, he already knows that likely, most of the first grade kids will pick one crayon. Those will end up drawing their entire picture with one color.

"Why didn't you choose any colors besides the black crayon?" He has asked many students something similar to that question and just gets a shrug of the shoulders.

"Why did you draw all of the people with only a brown pencil?" he once asked a student, and then turned red himself when he suddenly noticed the child was African-American.

Aartemann pays little homage to skin color except bronze suntan.

Aartemann always likes to mark Native American on forms asking for that consideration. He has no genealogy in that direction, only German and Irish, but he figures he is an American native, being born in the states after the Declaration of Independence, so he is a Native American. No one has ever cared or asked about it ... yet.

Aartemann gives the class the warning prep talk prior to lining them up for the walk from the art room to the courtyard. He likes to pretend it is something like a pep talk with an athletic team prior to the big game. It is to fire them up. It gives him feelings of power. It makes him think like a gym teacher. He wishes it gave him a tan.

"Okay kids. It's a nice day out, right?" No answer.

"Right?"

"Uh huh," is the pathetic reply from the troops, sounding more like a round robin song line for music class.

"How about drawing from nature, drawing a picture outside?"

"Yea!" Now he has their attention.

"We will walk to the courtyard. We will walk single file. We will not touch anything hanging in the hall. We will not talk in the hall. We will not run. We will not drop your paper or drawing board. We will not push. We will not get a drink on the way. We will not use the restroom. We will not hang from the light fixtures. These are your ten commandments," he finished as a testing to see if anyone was still listening.

A hand goes up.

"Yes, Ronnie," Aartemann acknowledges the hand.

"What is a cootyard?"

Mr. Aartemann does very well. He stands quietly for a moment's pause and does not laugh, not even a snicker.

"Courtyard. A courtyard is the area down the hall that is surrounded by the school building but it does not have a roof. It is almost like being outside. It is being outside. There are trees, and flowers, and bushes, and birds, and butterflies, and bugs, and grass, and rocks and benches, and all sorts of things to draw from nature. You are to make up your own picture from whatever you can see to draw. Don't forget to add the right texture to the objects you draw to make them look more real. You should try to use the real colors found on the real objects. You need to stay on the grass or on the stone walk or you may sit on a bench. Do not get in the water. Do not climb the trees. Do not pick the flowers for your mother. No swimming, did I say that? Ready? Line up please."

The class, some literally, jumps to their feet as excited about going outside as the teacher. They form typical lines, two. Not single file, but the students line up with boys in one line and the girls in another. They arrive this way to the art room and always, out of habit, do the same type of line to leave after art. Even with the instructions of a single file line, they focus in on their pattern of behavior.

"Okay, single file means only one line. Can you weave together, kind of like zipping a zipper?"

A hand goes up.

"Yes, Ronnie," Aartemann acknowledges the hand.

"What's a weeeve?" Ronnie draws out the word in question.

"Make one *straight* line," Aartemann at the helm suggests. "This one looks like a snake."

The line gets just a bit less serpentine.

"I wonder how many snakes are in the courtyard today," he teases. "We'll have to be on the look out for wild animals. This is a safari. It is a drawing safari."

A hand goes up.

"Yes, Ronnie," Aartemann acknowledges the hand.

"What's ah slafarii?" he butchers.

"A safari is a hunt. Usually it is a wild animal hunt.

But we're looking for things to draw. Maybe some wild animals, like a bird or a butterfly. Or maybe a ... *snake.*"

He pauses for effect.

"Or maybe, lions ... or tigers ... or bears ... oh, my, lions and tigers and bears, oh my, lions and tigers and bears, oh my," he chants softly as he begins to lead the class out into the hall toward their safari and his tan.

Lord, make this a memorable experience for all, he prays silently leading the class toward the destination near the office area.

Fortunately this time Mr. Aartemann took a look at the panic bar on the door prior to exiting the inside of the building and entering the courtyard area. The panic bar was locked. There is another door at the opposite end of the courtyard to reenter the building at that point but it is likely locked also. He finds the traditional stone, at a time like this as important as the Stone of Slone, lying beside the door on the outside. He kicks the granite chunk into the door jamb to make sure when all of the students are outside that the door will not completely close ... and *lock.*

He has been there before, entering the open spaces of the courtyard, having the door close behind, and the panic bar in the locked position. The class gets trapped inside the courtyard until someone comes by in the hall to assist by pushing the door open. Of course a key may be picked up at the office prior to entering the courtyard. But Mr. Aartemann is never that organized. Also there is the opportunity of knocking on the window of the principal's office, which is accessible since it faces the courtyard. He also would never consider doing that. Knocking exposes his stupidity to the principal. It is Aartemann pride at work as well. He would never live it down if he had to ask the principal. This principal is also a friend and one that can pour on the ridicule and teasing as heavily as Aartemann does to others at times.

Aartemann locked his class into the courtyard one time and spent almost a full ten minutes pounding on the windows toward the hall, trying to attract attention from a teacher, staff person, or a student. Finally after leaving fingerprints all over the glass as evidence of his goof, he was saved. Before the panic bar was pushed, releasing the door for the art class's escape back inside, at least a half dozen teachers and staff were standing in the hall laughing at the predicament. He has never, in ten years since, made the embarrassing mistake again.

Students spread out quickly in the courtyard, heading in all directions. The garden space is not extremely wide but it is as long as the building itself, with the exception of a hallway on each end of the courtyard. Aartemann rolls up the short sleeves of his shirt, wishing from deep inside that he is wearing a tank top, to collect sunrays. He finds a nice dry sunny spot on the edge of a raised platform. It is used as a stage for lectures on nature to other classes that use the few benches to sit, or stand on the stone paths. He sighs, contented as ol' Bossy the cow in a pasture knee high of annual rye. He keeps the tray of crayons next to him and students come and exchange colors as needed.

"Jarrod, move along," he shouts over to a student standing directly under a roof gutter opening that yesterday shot water onto plants and trees during the rain.

Today it has just a slow occasional drip from an apparent remaining standing pool of rainwater on the roof. Jarrod is letting the drips hit his head and go splat since he has hair cut to about a quarter inch length. Every once in a while he will look up and catch a drop on the forehead like Chinese water torture. "I'll bet the Chinese never did that at all," Aartemann says to himself while wondering in great puzzlement what is running through the mind of Jarrod.

"Tim! What you doing?" he speaks even as he jumps from his sunny perch and heads to the corner of the courtyard. A crabapple tree, good size, sits in the corner surrounded with large shrubs he cannot name. In front of a shrub is a drawing board book cover, a drawing start (all done in green), and Tim's head is all that is showing on the opposite side of the shrubs with his face toward the corner.

"What are you doing?" Aartemann questions Tim again.

"I gotta pee."

He says it so matter of factly that it has to be a natural thing to do at his house. He is not yet in the process, but Tim is preparing to relieve himself between the brick wall and the crabapple.

"Come on," Aartemann says as he gives a directional shake of his head in the "get out of there" indication.

Aartemann picks up the drawing and green crayon as he squeezes between the shrubs. Mr. Aartemann takes the lad lightly by the shoulder and escorts him to the door held open with the granite chunk and quietly says, with another directional shake of his head, "Hurry back! Don't run!"

Aartemann returns to the crayon tray location and retakes his sunny seat, finding next to it a tearful little girl named Trista. Trista Lista in total, and he never asked why on the name.

But now he asks, "What's the matter? It's too sunny a day for tears."

She is wiping her eyes with chubby little fists that are a bit mud soiled. Dirty fists spread marks like war paint on her cheeks. She doesn't even look up, but holds up her drawing with similar mud streaks and a pair of torn spots.

"No problem," he tells her, taking her paper. "Here's a new one, I have extras. There, is that better?"

She waits just a minute. That is all it takes to end the tears and find a smile. Selection of a new crayon is followed by her return to the flowerbed where she had toppled and torn her masterpiece, not to mention getting her fingers dirty.

A large group of artists have gathered around the fountain. The courtyard fountain consists of a small waterfall and a collection pool for the recycled water. Rocks surround the pool area that is not much more than about five or six feet in diameter. In season, tulips and then daylilies poke leaves and heads between rocks. Several nearby birdhouses are present in the courtyard, which attract nesters including a family of bluebirds every year. The crabapple tree supported a robin family for three years in a row from the same nest, until old man winter turned the nest into an Irish tumble-down. This next year, the nest is rebuilt by the robins in a maple tree at the opposite end of the courtyard.

Aartemann decides with such a large gathering around

the fountain that he also is interested in seeing how their pictures are progressing. He heads their way, leaving the crayon tray on the platform available for color changes, in case more than the three current exchangers decide upon something beyond a monochromatic naturescape.

"How are the pictures going?" he asks the crowd of at least ten artists gathered completely around the pool end of the fountain.

A couple more try hard to fill in sideways between kneeling Michelangelo's and Leonardo's.

"Cool!"

"Awesome!"

"Can we do this again?"

"See 'ow goo' my boid is?"

As Ronnie speaks, Aartemann thinks questioningly how he might have chosen to draw a bird by sitting all this time in front of water, flowers, and rocks. But then Ronnie is an exceptional child. He looks at the drawing.

"Yes, Ronnie, nice bird," he answers, twisting his head trying to make out the image and convert it into some sort of bird.

The drawing is all in black. The apparent rock, flower and bird images all seem much alike and all adorned with the same textures.

"Look at mine."

"See mine?"

"Is this good?"

Aartemann glances at other pictures done by students around the pool, as always some more successful than others. All seem to have a distorted bird image in the middle of a ring of rocks (the water area). He looks into the water at the student's model. Floating belly up is a bird. The eyes protrude from bloating along with the belly. Wings are spread like the bird is in a desperate struggle, using the backstroke for survival. The clawed feet, sticking straight for the sky, prove the failure of the struggle. Decomposition demonstrates a loss of life earlier than this day.

"Look, Mr. Aartemann, I even drew the flies on my bird. I bemembered how to do it from the fly project we had earlier in the year when we drew a new picture for the book by ..." (pause) " ... I don't bemember his name. I bemember the book was called 'Shoo fly! Shoo fly! Shooo' and I bemember you liked my fly that time. Bemember? Do you like mine?"

"Very nice, Marcus," he answers, looking wide-eyed.

Marcus is a smart student and always interested in details.

"The word is Remember, Marcus, Rr-remember. And the book was *Old Black Fly* by Jim Aylesworth, bemember? I mean, R-remember? The pages just ended with 'Shoo fly! Shoo fly! Shooo' and you read those words after I read the other words. Remember? Nice flies!"

Aartemann eyes the floating bird again and realizes it does have at least six large blue-black flies dining disgustingly.

"We really have to watch the fountain," the principal had shared with Aartemann another time in the year while they were both watching birds in the courtyard from the hallway windows. "The young birds stand on the plastic sides of the pool and reach over trying to get a drink and then topple into the water and drown. We try to keep them scooped out before students see them. I'd hate for the kids to see them."

"I guess it is a nature lesson, and half of the class is enjoying drawing the pool with its floater," he ponders as he tries to decide if he needs to remove the bird or the students.

He hears a snap and turns.

"Jennifer, down ... please," he gets out of his mouth just as the snapped limb falls completely away from the small tree and "Jungle Jenny" with it; still clinging tight. She lands in soft mulch six inches deep from a drop of only four feet. Actually, her drop is only a foot from feet to mulch. She sits staring; obviously knowing what she has done is against the procedures.

Aartemann returns to the sunny seat exhausted with natural art. He picks up an extra page and one color of crayon and begins his own drawing with a trio of girls sitting on the platform beside him. The students love to watch him draw. He closes his eyes for a minute and remembers drawing pictures in his own first grade classroom.

"What are you doing? You have not done the cow correctly. It is to be black, not brown. You have colored your whole cow brown. Look around you. Did anyone else use brown? No! Make sure you ..."

He remembers the nun scolding him for his cow. He didn't want a black cow. He wanted a brown cow. He thought it was better than all the rest. He liked making up his own pictures, not copying one from the board. What was wrong with his cow? He felt the sadness. He wondered why his teacher was a nun when he went to public school. He heard laughter. It was coming from first grade students. They were laughing at him.

Female first grade artists are at his side, looking at him and laughing, when Aartemann startles awake. He had fallen asleep in the warm sunshine. For how long, he wonders. He smiles, slightly embarrassed, and stands up.

"Line up on the stone walk," he announces to the class. "It's time to go back inside. Bring me your crayons and keep your drawings."

He is anxious to end this nature safari drawing lesson and all of the encountered lions and tigers and bears that are included in such a mistake.

He walks ahead of the class in the serpentine line returning to the art room. He lifts his rolled up short sleeve looking for any sign of a tan or even sunburn. He is as white as the eyes of the lifeless fountain floater. It has been a good lesson for … for Mr. Aartemann.

Saying an Art Room Goodbye

The end finally comes. Aartemann returns to his art room once more, alone. Nothing much is left to do since he's been packing boxes for weeks every time he recognized that something would not be needed again for this year. Next year all of the school books, tools, supplies and furnishings of the art room would be moved to another location or disposed of. The contents of the art room sit on the floor in boxes stacked in a manner resembling an old civilization that used pyramids for ending times. Today this art room is ending life as it has been known for over eighty years. This building will no longer be used. Likely torn down. He'll be leaving this building also. His choices are full retirement or relocation to a school of his choosing, due to restructuring of the art program and his seniority.

The investigation into a one semester job for the following year was turned down as an alternative. He'd gotten the information just this morning during the breakfast he did attend. He was not only told that that situation was rejected, but he was encouraged to consider taking a position for another year in the new building that is just being completed. The superintendent even told Aartemann he was sorry his name was not allowed to be placed into nomination for Teacher of the Year.

"Can you let me know your final decision on a school or retirement by the end of the day?" he asks Aartemann.

The art teacher affirms with a nod since suddenly his silent voice feels a bit choked. The moment of decision has arrived and Aartemann has cold feet, retirement fear, intense wavering, or at least major indecision. For an obvious reason, the superintendent approached him openly at the close of the breakfast. A choice is needed in haste.

"You didn't tell me about the nomination," Abs states.

She and Aartemann had arrived at the same time for the breakfast and sat together. Now they are the only two remaining at the table of six. She knows not to ask Aartemann about the retirement decision. They had talked much during the past two weeks and she is aware he is now more undecided than ever about ending his career and giving up time with students. She has seen many other retiring teachers go through the same turmoil.

"Just a bad decision on the principal's part. I'm not award material."

"The superintendent doesn't think so. Neither do your art students. Neither do I."

"Yeah, well, I've got one last box to pack and then I'm off. Probably won't see you later. You take care and if Paul mistreats you, anytime, call me, okay?"

"Sure."

She speaks as Aartemann gets up and turns away, swallowing harder than before.

"Hey, curmudgeon ..." she pauses when he stops.

"Thanks!"

Aartemann doesn't look back. He hears and then walks on.

———————

He sits down in the old oak straight back chair, a teacher's chair without arms, designed to match the desk. It is a hard seat, with carved cheek cups, but still a terrible chair and one he did not use when teaching in this room. He had purchased his own desk chair many years ago. Only the principal of a school gets to choose a chair for their desk, perhaps maybe the school secretary, and maybe, but not likely, the school counselor. A teacher gets what is left over from the original purchased equipment, and that is an antique oak chair in this building. It will be left behind when this school closes along with most of the furnishings. Only books and supplies will be moved. The chair will be replaced in the new building under construction, now almost finished. That place will have all new teacher desks purchased with an accompanying chair. The chair will likely be hard plastic, not hard oak. That is the progress that has taken place in teacher chairs since eighty-four years ago when this building was built and equipped.

The plastic chair will never last eighty-four years. Hard chairs are from an era where teachers were allowed the use of a wooden ruler to slap the palms of students' hands for chewing gum. That punishment has, fortunately, been outlawed. Hard teacher chairs have not. The catalog even lists the hard bottom chairs as teachers' chairs. Go figure!

The matching blonde varnish oak desk has likely been

in the school since its construction over four score years ago. The center drawer, over two feet wide above the knee cavity for sitting, has a lock. It is brass, still in place exactly in the center of the drawer. The brass holds a delightful greenish-grackish-grungish-brownish patina from years of lack of use due to the fact that the key has been missing for all the years that Aartemann used the desk. The preceding teacher told him that she had never had a key. Therefore the key was likely lost sometime in the first half of the desk's lifetime. He had gone through the desk when he boxed up his own personal things. But for sentimental reasons, he feels the need to open that drawer, the only one used often each day, one more time. He pulls it slowly, not remembering if he had emptied it or if he had left remainders. It is a bit like looking in a garage cabinet for the first time in spring after avoiding the garage workbench all winter long.

There is an eraser he remembers leaving behind because it is hard. It no longer will erase. It is a Pink Pearl eraser that must have been a chunk of one left over from a prior teacher, according to its petrified stiffness.

I'll bet it will shatter if I hit it with a hammer, he thinks to himself. He could speak aloud as he talks to himself like he does when alone, because no other person is around to hear. But the occasion is solemn. His return is for one last look at a room in a school where he has spent many years. It will no longer be used, and the building likely demolished. It is the throwing out of the old and ushering in of the new. He feels old.

In the drawer is an aluminum ring. It is blue and the

gray of raw aluminum with beading on the edge and dia-
mond shaped cuts around the center of the band. Surely
not cut diamonds like the girl that lost the ring probably
envisioned. He never found its owner. Now that seems
sad. It will be buried when the walls fall into the desk.
Three well-used pencils, needing sharpening, are visible
and none have erasers remaining. One of the pencils, a
blue one, holds teeth marks, probably not his.

The drawer still holds a yellow plastic whistle strung
with an old gym shoelace. It has no pea, the reason it is
abandoned. Mr. Aaretmenn holds it up as though confront-
ing the sadness of its end to usefulness and chuckles while
saying to himself, "I know what it's like needing a pea!"

There is a tiepin back, but no pin. The ink pen, void
of a cap, he passes over without even trying it to see if it
will write. The right side of the drawer has a crack in the
bottom of the drawer with a paper clip caught between
the bottom and the right side. A pair of thumbtacks lay
head down with the pins sticking up looking like stiff legs
of something dead. Dead like the room. There is yet a
partially used bottle of White-Out, likely worn out, and a
half billfold size picture of himself from school pictures of
some year long ago. Teachers always get a free set. He had
more hair then. An ugly tie.

"That is best left buried with the whistle," he says.

On the wooden bottom of the drawer are written a
couple of notes. There is a dollar amount without telling
what for, a name perhaps of a former teacher, and a phone
number. He remembers writing the phone number himself only about three years earlier. Because of the note, he

always has the number of the local flower shop to call in an order for his wife. She likes roses, but he usually orders a mixed variety of kinds that will last longer in a vase.

A wood writing board slides out just under the desktop on both sides of the center drawer and he opens both at once. The left still holds the last art class schedule from the current school year just finished. The Xeroxed page is Scotch taped down all the way around and is padded underneath by the previous year's schedule taped over the previous year's schedule over another year and yet another. The history of the school's art education scheduling is stacked on the writing slab. He slides the board back into hiding as he thinks of some of the horrible schedules with nine art classes per day and back to back art classes with no time to put away or get out supplies in between. He remembers such busy schedules, void of teacher preparation time, and even a break to "get the pea from the whistle." He laughs aloud at what he has just said aloud. It echoes once.

The right board is replaced as well, with only spots of paint, cuts from X-acto knives' work, pen marks, and other working marks left from moments not recallable to his brain.

The right drawers are empty, with the exception of dust and dirt. The left three drawers look similar except for the center, which has a half melted Lifesaver candy, red, stuck to the wood bottom. In the back hides a blue M&M peanut candy covered with dirt from rolling around every time the drawer is opened. He never did like the blue M&Ms ever since they came out with the new color. He never truly believed it won the election of the public. It has to be a Mars executive color conspiracy selection. He hasn't had an M&M all day but it doesn't tempt him—much.

The top of the desk is filled with marks that he hopes someone will sand out someday in salvaging the old antique oak desk. It seems today that it will be trashed. The desktop can tell stories. He remembers wiping a few tears off the wood during sad private times in the room. He feels some of that sadness returning to him off the oak he stares at. He shutters. He gets up quickly. He avoids where his memory starts to travel.

The four-foot high wall of filled boxes ready for moving to the new school location are already partially moved. The old round kiln near the wall that had been buried in the boxes, now stands alone, surrounded with dust balls. The kiln is dead. It does not work right and is not to be moved for further use, like the desk. They will be buried later with no stone monument marking their years of service. That makes Mr. Aartemann sad. His hard day is getting harder.

He is sadder about his desk than the kiln. He never did like teaching clay to elementary students. Every art teacher has horror stories of kiln projects turning into monster events that can rival Armageddon. Once a pinch pot, not dry enough prior to the firing, exploded in the kiln. It sat on a lower shelf directly beside a shelf pillar. The mini explosion of the clay moved the shelf pillar enough to cause that shelf to topple along with the domino effect of the three additional shelves over it. Over half of the projects from seven classrooms were cracked, broken, or glazed together in mass huddling by the time the kiln could be opened. Many second graders and first grade students shed tears over their little pots. Mr. Aartemann shed more than one for them also.

He remembers again the baseball bat smashing of a couple of his college clay attempts. The dried green ware pots were swatted by the professor that determined them unworthy of glaze. That is probably the real reason he never did like doing ceramic work with students. There are sure a lot of reasons why Mr. Aartemann could use some counseling. Teaching is like that. It is one of the highest stress related jobs according to some reports. Teachers stressfully write most of those reports, obviously.

Aartemann's faith has served as his counselor most days of his career.

Today is stressful. He will be glad when he is rid of teacher stress. He fights a tear and his eye swallows it without shedding. He walks past the kiln, looks up and notices the five wires crisscrossed across the art room from attached points on the ceiling. He thinks of all of the art projects that have hung from those wires. Those wires made a multitude of students proud of their work. It is one of the joys that Mr. Aartemann has always considered a perk to teaching. Teachers do not get two hour paid lunches, gas charge cards paid by the company, company cell phones, or Christmas bonuses. Teacher perks are getting to see broad smiles when a fourth grade student walks into art and sees the project just completed hanging from a wire over their table where it was created. A perk is getting a drawing given to the art teacher because the child is so very proud of their work. But unfortunately they know it will get no praise at home. Some never even get refrigerator hang time. Mr. Aartemann gets a thrill in having a student thank him for choosing their picture for the bulletin board or for a library art display.

The wires look sad today. But they have in the past brought so much joy to so many students.

Above the picture wires are six very large and very heavy radiators, relics of the ancient heating system. Monster boilers actually ceased doing their job before the school's heating season ended. One of two boilers failed completely and with a new building underway, funds were not wasted on a boiler replacement. Repairs failed. One boiler did not do adequate work for the entire building to be comfortable. The art room got the first of the hot water and needed open windows in winter to regulate the heat to an acceptable minimum. Upstairs students worked math and read in sweatshirts and coats.

The art room has no thermostat; it could not be repaired so it was bypassed to a constant on. Thus the needed cracked windows in winter provided Mr. Aartemann with another perk, in-classroom refrigeration for his bottle of club soda. Sometimes in really cold weather it would crystallize and become a club soda slushy. He drinks it plain, like bottled water. Soda, drank straight, makes him in the eyes of some, again suspect regarding sanity.

The eighty-four year old radiators suspended from the ceiling, likely weighing a half-ton each, have no fewer than fourteen drip catching devices spread throughout the room. They lingered directly over students. They gave him much concern. Some have rusted joints at valves that drip into cans so rusted themselves they are beginning to drip in tandem. The cans are void of labels but likely food tins at one time. Rustily they demonstrate several decades, surely, of leaks never satisfactorily repaired. Two places that have the fresher leak beginnings have a plastic bucket hanging rather than a tin can. The buckets are gray plastic mimicking the galvanized buckets of Aartemann's youth.

A similar bucket is located under the sink unit to the east and holds a can of spray, a soft cloth, and a yellow sponge. The buckets were distributed to teachers a few years back when it was decided that custodians could not keep up. Funds were not available to hire additional help to work a building falling in such repair need. Thus chalkboard cleaning could be a teacher assignment. It brought on lots of comments from teaching staff like: "I failed chalkboard cleaning class," or "It's not in my job description," or "Which end again is the top of the sponge?" or "I don't think so," and a few other lines more savage than clever.

Aartemann's bucket is yet to be used. He did discover the sponge, when dry, cleans a chalkboard better than the erasers the school purchases, and refuses to have anyone clean. He can remember when he was a boy in elementary hoping to be chosen for the eraser cleaning duty. That person got to take the erasers outside and beat them against the brick wall till the dust was all off the erasers. Unfortunately the dust was usually found in the hair, ears, face, and clothing of the volunteer student worker.

Once when a meeting of the staff was organized with

school board members and high administrative staff, teachers got a chance to offer reasons why a new school was needed. It would be necessary to sell the idea to the taxpayers if it was to happen, it had been reasoned. Mr. Aartemann tried to share the situation in his room with the hot water pipes leaking overhead and wrapped with asbestos insulation. He shared his concern that one of the joints might let go directly over a group of students and scald them. The asbestos hazard they already knew about and ignored for the most part. It was explaining the potential of scalded students that sent his voice quivering, his eyes misting, and suddenly ended his presentation of art room need. He was unable to compose himself for further details, which greatly embarrassed him at the time. Seeing the cans intending to catch the leaks brought no sadness on this day. In a new building, no dangerous leaky rusty heavy pipes will adorn the art room ceiling. Kids will be safe.

"Praise God!" he says aloud at that thought.

He laughs to himself, but out loud, when he begins considering using the desk and reaching up to the asbestos pipe wraps. He considers tearing a chunk from the pipes, having it entombed in a block of clear plastic, like those rose encased paperweights, and hanging it over his new art room—just for auld lang syne. Aartemann catches himself and wonders why he just said to himself "*His* new art room."

Another ten inches above the eight-inch diameter pipes wrapped with the less than healthy asbestos wrap is the cement ceiling. In places it looks like it is covered with spider webs, and likely it is, but the truly visible lines looking like cobwebs are really cracks. They are the same cracks that were there when he first started in this school, this room. They seem to be stable cracks if a crack can be any kind of stable.

He used to make up stories of explanation to his classes. They were total lies, so wild they rivaled Disney cartoons. No matter how far-fetched a story is, some young mind will accept it as the gospel just because their art teacher said it was so. It is a responsibility an elementary teacher has to remember.

He recalls, "That crack was made by a student that got an A on the very project you are beginning today. She was so excited about getting an A that she began jumping up and down, higher and higher, until her head hit the ceiling with such a boom that the ceiling cracked. Her head fell off and bounced four times in the direction of the door and would have rolled all the way down the hall to the restroom had it not been for the wastepaper can that I picked up and threw overhand putting a spin on the toss, like you guys do with a football, and it landed over her head and trapped it just as it tried to bounce out the door. We used masking tape and put her head back on but we could not fix the crack in the ceiling. And that is why I never give letter grades in art any longer, just number grades, or plusses and checks. Okay, how many of you believe that story?"

Two hands appear from grinning students.

"Well, okay, I lied. I used a butterfly net to catch the head, not the waste can. Okay, I lied again. It was duct tape not masking tape … or was it Scotch tape? Okay, that's a lie too. I made it all up. I'm sorry! Forgive me!"

And they laugh and giggle. But when they line up to leave, and their teacher arrives for an escort back to their classroom, some try to fill her in on the story. Some must actually believe parts of it.

"My son visited last year. He is really tall. He forgot and tried to stand up. Ouch, that left a mark."

This year when he really did surprise Aartemann with a walk-in visit, a student stared at his height, and truly believed. He could see it in her eyes.

In the corner of the room to the northeast, where two or three cracks can be seen meeting, is a rich variegated umber and burnt sienna toned stain in the cement about the size of a bushel basket. Prior to placing electronic eye flushers on the stools and urinals in the restrooms, students every year figured out that in the restroom, a boys' restroom, directly above, the top of the stool tank was suspended eight feet up the wall (an ancient tank design) and it had no lid. Students would make balls from toilet tissue and throw them into the tank till there was enough to stop up the works inside. They would then do a few multiple flushes and return to class. The tank would overflow with nobody around till the next student needed to use the necessity. It would flow and flow. Flowing to the floor seeking its own level. The mini river would go through the cracks and bless the art room with its final resting place.

Over the years, accounting to the brown patina on the cement ceiling, other forms of stoppage and overflowing also took place. The water was not always fresh. That corner was always avoided when furniture placing was considered.

Mr. Aartemann remembers anew the addition to the school of the automatic flush devices. He snickers. He recalls the concept of the first semester kindergarteners using the urinals down the hall. The old fixtures were vintage, being over four foot tall, floor embedded, with Sloan valves at the top. The handles were replaced on the Sloan valves with the electronic eyes. Most new kindergarten boys are not four feet tall. He wondered all the time if they had to use the relief facility by standing at the urinal with their hands in the air, looking more like a person being robbed at gunpoint. In that way when they finished and headed to the sinks the urinal would flush. They would not be tall enough to even have their head do the electronic eye flushing.

He laughs out loud and it echoes across the art room as he again pictures ten kinder boys lined up (for there are ten urinals) with their trousers at their ankles and their hands raised in surrender to the beams. The thought makes some of the sadness pass as he continues the final lap of the room.

He comes upon "the" outlet directly under the speaker box. Between them is the projection screen hanging on a pair of large shelf brackets that had been mounted just above the chalkboard. The chalkboard is one of the newest additions to the room, even though it was added prior to his arrival for teaching in the room. It is not the old fashioned slate board that still exists in some of the rooms. They come complete with a built in oak chalk tray. This is a modern aluminum framed smooth black board that holds magnets for hanging examples and completed with an aluminum chalk tray. It is still holding short pieces of white and yellow chalk. He looks upon one abandoned eraser that is not a sponge, and chalk dust thick enough in the chalk tray to prove he never cleans the board or tray.

He'll never be able to explain why he is doing it. After he's done he'll check the hall to make sure no other person is around. He picks up the old dirty chalkboard eraser and pounds it over and over, again and again, harder and harder against the brick wall beside the doorway. He whiffs off to his old elementary for a spell. He cleans for the first, last, and only time, an eraser of the art room. He does it just like he was taught when he was an elementary student, only he didn't take it outside. He backs away from the cloud of dust it makes, and the body movement sucks the cloud toward his direction of movement. A belly laugh erupts from him. It is visible in the chalk cloud. He throws the eraser across the room and hits the abandoned dead kiln making the eraser gasp one last white puff.

"Don't throw things in the art room!" he shouts, pretending to address an unruly student.

He laughs again and goes to the door and checks for any undesirable witness. Aartemann leaves the dust stamp on the wall looking like a valuable Miro art piece.

He shakes his head one last time at the placement of the projection screen directly over the only outlet in the art room. That was probably some executive decision as to where the outlet and the screen were placed. It likely was written up in carbon triplicate in the days before NCR paper. To use any projection equipment an extension cord has to be run across the room, across student tables. How simple it should have been to decide to mount the screen across the room from "the" outlet. It is the only electrical outlet in the entire room. The exception is the 220 line brought in for the use of the dead kiln, which surely was not terminal when installed.

"Never again," he mutters quietly causing again a bit of sadness to enter a heart not sure what direction to go—sad or glad. "Never again!"

Never will this screen again see him doing his silly hand shadows in the beam while he waits for a designated student to turn off the lights. And this room will hold no future students to watch him stand in front of the overhead projector and turn on the switch lighting up the beam directly in his face. He mimes the movement as though a class is sitting in the room. He raises his hands in front of his face, jumps backward like it is the headlight of a locomotive, and peaks between fingers looking for laughs from the students. But the students are ghosts. In retirement he'll hear no more student laughs.

"Never again," this time he says aloud, turning from the student mirage with the heart scale tipped heavier on the sad side.

He looks up to pull down the screen one more time and spots the speaker box above. It is a brown-varnished wood box about a foot square with a cloth insert over the hidden inside speaker. The wood cutout backed by the cloth is in the form of a circle with a curved Y shape dividing the circle hole into three equal parts. Dust buildup from years of use is a cap. A wire leads from the box across the wall above the chalkboard. The faded brown cord hangs from bent nails like a telephone line draped from one pole to the next. At the end is a small metal box containing a little push call button designed to alert the office of the need for communication. He seldom uses it. The speaker box is also directly linked to a speaker box on the other side of the wall, which is in a teacher-only area, former teacher lounge. They share the same wire to the two speakers, thus shared is the same communication whether it is meant for there or the art room.

It is the only shared wire for speaker boxes in the school. That could supposedly be considered a unique award.

"It is also a unique annoyance," he announces to the empty walls.

"Who cares, it is only a problem when I'm trying to lecture and a conversation is taking place with someone in there. And we can only hear the office half of the conversation," he states to himself trying to reassure himself that the art program is more than just a half considered token subject area in his school.

"Never again, I should be saying 'It *was* only a problem' because it will never happen again," he falls back into silent thoughts that align with something surpassing sadness.

The moment is heading to an emotion level of grief. A classroom death, a kiln death, an eraser and desk about to be buried with life yet in them, creates for an old art man a mild form of grief. It is a passing. It is his passing.

He wipes the tear that embarrasses him even though he is alone. He turns, coughs once, and heads back to the door. He stops for just a second and salutes the chalk Miro on the golden brown brick bound with black mortar. The white of the mortar is blackened with the dirt of eighty-four years of use.

Never again, he thinks as he exits a finale. No one hears the sobs nor sees the tears splash on the once waxed-now scuffed cement floor because he composes himself prior to climbing the stairs to the school's exit.

Aartemann stops in at the office, hands the secretary his key and asks, "Okay to use the phone in the nurse's office?"

He takes a longer time than needed looking up a phone number because he is silently praying about what he is about to do.

"Lord, I've asked for Your direction, You today seem to show me a direction, so now Lord, if this decision is not Your perfect will, stop it now. I choose to serve your perfect will for this time in my life and always."

Aartemann neither says nor thinks an "Amen." He dials. Someone, he misses the name, answers politely and professionally.

"This is Mr. Aartemann, the art teacher. May I talk to the superintendent, please?"

"Yes, just a minute, he has been expecting your call. I'll transfer you to his line."